MOB TIES

SAYNOMORE

**Lock Down Publications and Ca$h
Presents**
MOB TIES
A Novel by *SAYNOMORE*

SAYNOMORE

Lock Down Publications
P.O. Box 944
Stockbridge, Ga 30281
www.lockdownpublications.com

Copyright 2021 SAYNOMORE
Mob Ties

Lock Down Publications
Like our page on Facebook: Lock Down Publications @
www.facebook.com/lockdownpublications.ldp
Cover design and layout by: **Dynasty Cover Me**
Book interior design by: **Shawn Walker**
Edited by: **Leondra Williams**

Stay Connected with Us!

Text **LOCKDOWN** to 22828 to stay up-to-date with new releases, sneak peaks, contests and more...

Thank you!

Submission Guideline.

Submit the first three chapters of your completed manuscript to ldpsubmissions@gmail.com, subject line: Your book's title. The manuscript must be in a .doc file and sent as an attachment. Document should be in Times New Roman, double spaced and in size 12 font. Also, provide your synopsis and full contact information. If sending multiple submissions, they must each be in a separate email.

Have a story but no way to send it electronically? You can still submit to LDP/Ca$h Presents. Send in the first three chapters, written or typed, of your completed manuscript to:

LDP: Submissions Dept
P.O. Box 944
Stockbridge, Ga 30281

DO NOT send original manuscript. Must be a duplicate.

Provide your synopsis and a cover letter containing your full contact information.

Thanks for considering LDP and Ca$h Presents.

Acknowledgments

First, I would like to thank God and my Lord and Savior Jesus Christ for all the blessings in my life and all the hard times for walking me thru them.

Much respect and love goes out to the Lockdown Publication family for believing in me. Big shout-out goes out to Ca$h, hands down , respect and love, bruh!

I want to Thank my mother, Rafanella, and my auntie mother, Evada, for everything in my life. Also, my auntie Nan for loving me unconditionally, I love you, beautiful! I want to Thank my sister, Alisha "Sweet pea" Medlin for helping me reach out to Lockdown Publications. I want to thank my children's mother, Barbara aka. "Babz". I want to thank all of my children: Charmmorro, Jataya, Jelani, and Sharese Jr. for loving me unconditionally because y'all pushed me to be a better father. Much love to my sister, Destiny, and my brother, Molif, Jaja and Nyaisha. Much respect goes out to Sidney aka "T- ville" McKinney, Jr. for rocking with me from day one. Mad love and respect goes out to Jodrian "Slim Boogie" Griffis, Jeff "PBN" Anderson, Lester " Badii" Parrish, Diante "Kao$" Boatman, Antonio "Young boy" Jr. Elvis "Honduras" Garcia, Norris "Playa Ray" McCoy, Rueben "Oso" Almaguer, Raymond Clark, George Jackson, Randall "Big Ru" Jones, Kodak, Boo, Nitty, Have, Hollywood, Dw, Triple O, Murda Mu, Quick , JB, Thugga, Big Suaver, and Eric " Perk G" Perkinson.

Timmy aka Jr. My brother Molefe.

SAYNOMORE

Chapter One

Jamila was sitting at her desk looking at a picture of her and Fabio that they took when he took her to Paris for the very first time. She remembered he told her he loved her that night. Her thoughts were interrupted by the ringing of her phone.

"Hello, Mrs. LaCross, a Mr. Frankie Landon just arrived and asked me to inform you that he is here."

"Ok, thank you. Have someone see him to the bar and let him know I'll be down shortly."

"Yes, Mrs. LaCross."

Jamila opened her top right desk draw and took out her black 9mm and placed it in her Versace bag. She closed the desk drawer and made her way through her office doors to meet Frankie.

"Mr. Landon, would you like something to drink until Mrs. LaCross arrives?"

"Yes, gin on the rocks," Frankie responded.

Frankie looked around Jelani's. He hasn't been there in over six months since the wars started. Jamila saw Frankie from across the room at the bar having a drink. She stopped at the front desk to let the manager know she would be gone for the rest of the day. She walked up to Frankie and gave him a kiss on the cheek and his bodyguard Marcus a light hug.

"So, Jamila, where is it that you are taking me today?"

"Just for a ride no more than twenty minutes away from here."

"Where is Lorenzo at?"

"Waiting on us."

Jamila had two armed bodyguards with M-16's waiting for her next to her limousine. After getting in, Frankie spoke. "Jamila, it's not very smart to be riding around. A war is going on."

"Frankie, I have two cars with us. One in front of us and one behind us. If Sammy's going to make a move, let him. There's nothing that me or you can do to stop him. Isolation is dangerous plus history shows us anybody can get killed."

Frankie nodded his head as he reached in his pocket and pulled out a lighter and a Cuban Cigar. He lit it and took a long pull before speaking. "You are right."

The limousine turned down a dirt road with trees on both sides. Frankie looked out the window and saw dead men tied to the trees and wild dogs eating at them. He looked at Jamila and she just smiled at him. He looked again out the window and saw a big field. It looked like a rundown farm that hadn't been used in years. The limousine came to a stop and Jamila's door opened. Her, Frankie and Marcus stepped out. She had two bodyguards waiting to walk her to Lorenzo through the barn. Frankie looked at Marcus. "Have you ever been here before?"

"No, I haven't."

"Jamila, what is this place?" asked Frankie.

"A place where nobody wants to come, and I get answers at. Follow me."

When they started walking through the barn, you saw a man tied to a tree with a bag over his head. Lorenzo saw Jamila and walked up to her and gave her a kiss on both cheeks and then shook Frankie and Marcus's hand. Jamila looked at Lorenzo and said.

"Have someone put a few chairs over there for me, Frankie and Marcus. Is he talking yet?" asked Jamila.

Lorenzo looked at Jamila and said, "Not a word."

"Ok, have somebody bring the dogs out also."

Jamila walked up to the man tied to the tree and pulled the bag off his head. Frankie was shocked when he saw Sunnie's face. He had blood coming from his lips and black and blue marks over his face. Jamila looked back at Frankie and then looked at Sunnie and said, "How you die today is up to you. I'm walking in a pair of $3000 dollar stiletto shoes in the dirt just to see how strong your loyalty is today."

Jamila walked over to Frankie and he asked her, "How long has he been here for?"

Two days now. Lorenzo caught him and his guys leaving a bar in downtown Manhattan."

"Where are his guys at now?" asked Frankie.

"Dead on the trees tied up. You saw them on the way here. Frankie, they ripped a hole in my heart that can never be filled again. I'll kill them all in the worst way."

"I know your pain Jamila."

Jamila walked back over to Sunnie and looked at him and said, "Where the fuck is Sammy at?" Sunnie looked at her and spat blood on her shoes. Jamila nodded her head and told Lorenzo to strip him down to his boxers and to cut his right ear off. Lorenzo put on a pair of black gloves and walked up to him with a box cutter. He lifted his head up, placed it behind his ear and sliced his ear off. All you heard and saw was Sunnie yelling out of pain and blood all over his face. Then Lorenzo cut his clothes off.

Jamila walked up to Sunnie and said, "I have your wife and kids also. Your ID gave me the address. Should I bring them out to see how strong your loyalty really is?"

Sunnie looked at Jamila with blood covering his face and said, "Fuck you."

"You see those dogs over there? Let's play a game." Jamila walked over to Frankie and told Lorenzo to let them loose on him. "But first, untie him from the tree." When Sunnie's body hit the ground, both dogs jumped on him. Sunnie was screaming out of pain as the dogs started ripping his meat off his arms and legs down to the bone. Frankie looked at Jamila and Marcus and he couldn't believe what he was witnessing. He looked at Jamila and said, "Stop this. He's not going to talk."

She looked at Frankie and said, "They all talk at some point."

Jamila told Lorenzo to pull the dogs off him. She then got up and walked over to Sunnie. She looked at him lying on the ground bleeding and said, "Sunnie, where is Sammy's whereabouts or this will happen to your daughter next."

Sunnie said with broken words and pain in his voice, "215 Rock Lane Drive."

"Thank you. I'll keep your wife and child just for insurance. And if that's right, I'll let them go."

Jamila pulled out her black 9mm and placed it to Sunnie's head and fired two shots. His body went limp. She looked at Lorenzo and said, "burn his body." She then looked at Frankie and said, "Shall we go now?"

Chapter Two
Eight Months Earlier...

Fabio looked at Tony and Sammy in the eyes and said, "I'm not paying you or anybody else 30% of my restaurant or 40% of my cocaine sales. I'm not scared of you, Tony. Everyone else might be but I'm not."

Tony looked at Fabio and said, "Out of respect for your late mother and father and you being my godson, I'm having great patience with you. Fabio. Everyone pays dues."

"My mother and father are dead. It was a conversation just like this they had with you and two days later they got killed. That was 14 years ago," said Fabio.

I told you my hands were clean of that, Tony said. "I know they were but, what about Sammy or Sunnie over there?"

Sammy looked at Fabio and said, "If it was up to me, I would have been cut your fucking throat from ear to ear."

Tony looked at Sammy and said, "I got this. Fabio is your mind made up?"

"Yes, it is, and Sammy whenever you are ready you know where to find me." Fabio sat at the table with his legs crossed as Tony smoked his cigar. Looking at him he said, "My product, my money, my cocaine sales. I have people I pay to let my product come in the states and to keep law enforcement off my back."

Tony looked at Fabio and said, "don't make the same mistake your father and mother made. We're talking $30,000 a month and what's your gross income a month? $300,000 or $400,000?"

Fabio looked at Tony and said, "With all due respect, I believe this conversation is over."

Tony stood up and fixed his tie and said, "Just because I'm your Godfather, don't mean I will treat you differently. There's a meeting with all the families next month in Brooklyn. Be there."

"I'm not a gangster or a mobster Tony. So why do I have to be there?" said Fabio.

"Because I said so." Tony looked at Sammy and Sunnie they both got up and they all walked out the door.

Fabio looked at them as they left and said to himself. "There's a box waiting for you too, Tony."

Fabio looked out the restaurant windows with his hands behind his back at the spot his mother and father were killed at. Flashbacks of the car being shot up with over one hundred rounds with three men who jumped out the back of a UPS truck wearing all black with AK-47's. His mother, father and driver were all pronounced dead on the scene. It was all over the news the killing of Paul LaCross and wife Jessica. It was an assassination that no one could save them from. His mother and father had closed caskets because the bodies were beyond recognition. The last words his father told him was, "Never back down and stand your ground."

Fabio was eighteen years old when his mother and father were killed. His father's longtime friend took him under his wings. Frankie Landon took Fabio and showed him the drug game firsthand. After eight years when Frankie could no longer supply him, he introduced him to Morwell, a Mexican drug lord. Fabio became his number one client.

Fabio sold more drugs in Queens, NY than anyone. He was letting kilos go for $25,000 when everyone else was letting them go for $40,000. If you wanted to cook up, he had them for $18,000. You had dealers coming from all over New York City to shop with him. He had four five-star restaurants to wash his money through. One in New York and three in Paris all called Jelani. He never put a name on his organizations because he knew once he did that, the Feds step in and then its organized crime.

There were three of them; Cordial, who was thirty-one years old. He was Spanish and grew up in Spanish Harlem. The females loved him. He knew the streets and had a lot of pull in them. He was light skin with green eyes, stood five foot nine, with long dark hair.

Then he had Tesfar, a thirty-four-year-old Jamaican. He was from southside Jamaica Queens, best known for killing. He was dark skin, long locs, brown eyes. He stood six foot one, with white smile but don't let his smile fool you. You could tell he worked out.

Then there was Fabio. He was thirty-three years old who was French with curly blond hair, hazel eyes, standing five foot nine and was slim. Fabio walked over to his bird cage and pulled out his cell phone and called Tesfar. With a deep Jamaican accent, Tesfar picked up.

"Yo man."

"We need to talk, come to the restaurant and make sure you have Cordial with you."

"What time?"

"Be here within thirty minutes. I'm on my way."

Fabio knew there was only a matter of time before a war started and he needed to be ready. Fabio was on the phone when Tesfar and Cordial walked in.

"Frankie, let me call you back. Ok I will."

"What's up Fabio, what's the word?" asked Cordial.

"Tony and two of his goons pulled up on me today."

"What did he want?" Cordial asked.

"30% of the restaurant and 40% of everything else."

"And what you tell him?" That this conversation is over.

Tesfar looked at Fabio and said, "Fuck them. Don't nobody put the press on us."

"We just got to stay strapped up," Cordial said.

"It's not always about the gun, Cordial."

"What happens when you run into someone with just as many guns you have or maybe even more?"

"Tony has everyone watching his back. Cops, judges, DA's, Mobsters. We have to outthink him."

"So, let's just give him the $30,000 a fucking month and be done with it?"

"Because Cordial over time he's going to want more. So, we need to stop it before it starts," Fabio said.

"Look there's a meeting he wants me to come to next month in Brooklyn."

Tesfar cut him off. "You go there you dead man."

"I need a drink," said Cordial.

"Let's go to Boy Boy's, have a few drinks and talk about this tomorrow."

"It's already 9:30p.m. Fuck it," Fabio said. "Let's go."

It was 10:30p.m when they walked in Boy Boy's. You had over 1000 people in there. The DJ was playing Jay-Z *Rock Boys* when he saw Fabio walking in the club. The DJ gave him a shout out and Fabio threw up his hand to him.

"Yo, this shit jumping tonight," said Cordial

"Facts. Let's go play the VIP," said Tesfar.

"Ya go get the VIP. I'm going to grab us some bottles of Ace of Spades and I'll meet ya up there," Fabio said.

Fabio walked to the bar.

"Hey beautiful," he said to the bartender.

"What can I get you handsome?"

"Let me get three bottles of Ace of Spades and have them bring them up to VIP, sexy.

"Ok I will have them brought up."

As Fabio walked off, he saw a light-skinned female wearing an Apple Bottom outfit with open toe red bottom shoes on. Her hair was in micro braids. She favored J. Lo. He walked up to her and said, "How are you doing tonight?"

Jamila looked at him from his blond hair and hazel eyes and white smile.

"I'm doing good tonight, so do you have a name?"

"Are you asking me if I have a name? Or asking me for my name, because there is a difference."

Fabio let out a smile and said, "I'm asking for your name?"

"My name is Jamila, and you are?"

"Fabio."

"Fabio?"

"Yes, that's it. Do you want to come with me to the VIP?"

"And why would I want to do that?"

"So I can get to know you."

"Why do you want to get to know me?"

"I'm just trying to vibe with you plus I like your style."

"And what about my friend over there?"

"Who?" Fabio asked.

"The one wearing the Baby Phat outfit."

"Yea, she can come too. What's her name?"

"Nayana."

"Tell her to come on."

"Ok, Mr. Fabio, I'll meet you up there."

"Don't have me waiting."

"I'll try not to."

Fabio looked at her one more time before walking off with a smile. Jamila walked over to Nayana and tapped her on the shoulder. When Nayana turned around she said, "Hey beautiful."

"What's up?"

"Look you see them guys up there in VIP?" Jamila said.

"Yea, I see them."

"They just invited us up there."

"Let's go."

"You sure?"

"Yea come on."

"Ok."

When they reached the VIP, Fabio grabbed Jamila's hand and said, "Come sit next to me."

Cordial looked at Nayana and said, "Come vibe with me over here."

Nayana smiled and said, "Ok and what's your name?"

"Cordial, and what's your name beautiful?"

"Nayana."

"I like the name. So where you from, beautiful?"

"183rd in the Bronx and you?"

"Spanish Harlem. Are you enjoying your night?"

"Yea, so far."

"So, you be in here a lot?"

"No, I'm just taking my home girl out tonight. What about you?"

"Yea, I come through here from time to time and kick back!" said Cordial.

"So, you come way out to Queens to kick back? What, you don't have no spots jumping in Spanish Harlem?"

"Yea, we got it rocking clubs be jumping, but Queens is my second home."

"I hear you. So, you just up here popping bottles?" asked Nayana.

"What, we can't enjoy the fruits of our labor?"

"And what is your labor?"

"Where that question come from?" Cordial said with a smile.

"What a bitch can't find out who she is sitting next too?" Nayana said with a jerk of her neck.

"I'm not saying that baby girl. Cool down. I'm a manager at a restaurant."

"Ok," Nayana said.

Nayana looked over at Jamila who looked like she was in a deep conversation with Fabio.

Chapter Three

"Would you like a drink, Jamila?" Fabio asked.

"Yes, I would like a long island iced tea." Fabio waived over the waiter and told her to bring a bottle of long island iced tea up to V.I.P with ice.

"Fabio, you know I only wanted a glass not a bottle."

"You might want another round," Fabio said, licking his lips.

Jamila lowered her eyes and said, "body language is 85% of a conversation."

"That's a true fact, but why you say that?" Asked Fabio.

"Because you all have bottles of Ace of Spades. You're not wearing a bunch of jewelry or diamond earrings. And when you talk to me, your eyes stay locked on mine."

"That's because you have my full attention and wearing a bunch of jewelry just makes you a target for hating as niggas in the streets, police, jack boys or a secret indictment." Fabio stated.

"So, you're telling me in so many words you are a drug dealer?" asks Jamila.

"I'm not telling you I'm a drug dealer. I'm telling you why I don't wear jewelry and look, your long island iced tea has finally arrived."

"Thank you and here you go," Fabio says to the waiter. "Shall we drink Jamila?"

Jamila looked at him and said, "Sure so what do you do Fabio?"

"I own a restaurant, what about you?"

"I'm a counselor," replied Jamila.

"Beautiful, bold and intelligent. So, what brings you out tonight?" asked Fabio.

"My friend Nayana corrupted me to come out with her tonight."

"So, Jamila, can I call you sometime or maybe take you out to eat?"

"Where is your phone at?" asked Jamila.

"Right here."

"Let me put my number in it. Be sure to call me, Mr. Fabio."

"I will."

"And thank you for the drink."

"You only had one glass."

"I told you that was all I wanted. Bye."

Cordial was telling Nayana something in her ear when Jamila said, "Come on girl."

Nayana looked at Cordial and said bye as they walked down the steps from the VIP room.

Jamila we were only up there for about twenty or thirty minutes. I know and now let them come for us Beautiful, Jamila said as they left.

Chapter Four

It was 1p.m Saturday afternoon.

"Tony, our family done spilled more blood in these streets than the Landon family, Gotti family, Gambino family and Dinero family. Everyone pays dues to us just to have a peaceful night's sleep. Who the fuck Fabio think he is? Just because you are his godfather don't mean shit. He is disrespectful and needs to be put in his place. They call you the untouchable Don, the Boss of Bosses. I remember we would send a fucking head in a box back to a family just to get a point across. Burn down buildings, kidnap wives and kids. Shit, there's bodies still out there that ain't been found because they fucked with us. I still hear muthafuckers screaming from the meat rack." Sammy said as he walked back and forth in Tony's office.

"Burn down Jelani's and put him in a black bag and be done with his ass. Send him to his mother and fucking father."

Tony took a pull of his cigar and said, "Sammy, I can't kill him. I already had his mother and father killed."

"I'm not telling you to kill him. I will." said Sammy.

"Sammy, we have a meeting in a few days. There we will tell him what the business is," replied Tony.

"Tony if we don't do something now someone else might try us and refuse to pay dues. $300,000 to $400,000 can be coming to us. Shit, I remember in the early 70's you gave his father $50,000 to start up that restaurant? You kept your end of the deal. They broke their end. And that's why they are dead now. Tony, I have more blood on my hands than anyone else in this family. You ask me to get it done with no questions asked, let me take care of the fucking flea and be done with it," said Sammy.

Tony got up and walked to his window. Without looking back at Sammy, he began speaking.

"We have the Mayoral election coming up within three weeks. Take care of it after the election. I don't need the police breathing down my neck. And I don't need the local news team in our business. Make it clean and don't let him feel any pain or suffering," said Tony.

"I won't," Sammy replied before walking out.

Tony knew Fabio wasn't going to show up to the meeting and Sammy was right. Tony couldn't afford to look weak to nobody. In his mind Fabio made his bed, now it's time for him to lay in it.

Chapter Five

Jamila's phone went off, she saw it was Lorenzo calling her.

"Hey, what's up Lorenzo?"

"I was seeing if you wanted to go to the shooting range today?"

"Yea, I'm up for that what time?" asked Jamila.

"How does 3 p.m. sound?" Replied Lorenzo.

"Good to me. I'll see you then."

"Cool."

After hanging the phone up, Jamila saw she had a text message from Fabio as well.

"I had a good night last night with the little bit of time we had together. I was wondering if we can have dinner tonight, around 8 p.m. If it's not too late."

Jamila replied back, "No that's fine with me, but I did promise Nayana I would spend the night with her. Can I bring her along with me?"

Within two minutes Fabio replied back and said, "Cordial can accompany her. We will see you then."

Jamila text Nayana and told her and they went to get ready to meet Lorenzo at the shooting range.

SAYNOMORE

Chapter Six

"So, Jamila. Nayana told me you went out last night."

"Yea, somehow I let her talk me into it. You know I don't do clubs Lorenzo."

"I know, that's why I was so surprised when she told me." said Lorenzo.

"I'm not all that boring Lorenzo. Anyway, let's see what your shooting game is like today."

"I'm willing to bet it's better than yours," Lorenzo stated.

"We will see Lorenzo."

After two hours at the shooting range, they went and got some sodas.

"So how you been, Lorenzo?" asked Jamila.

"You know me, making my next move my best move. How's work?" asked Lorenzo.

"Good, I can't complain. I don't have to work so many hours any more, so that gives me a chance to go to the gym. Tone up and catch up on my reading," replied Jamila.

"That's good to hear. It was nice seeing you. It's been like forever," said Lorenzo.

"It has not been that long."

"You right, but look I have some runs to make, Jamila, so I'll hit you up tonight."

"That's fine with me," Jamila says.

"Take care."

"You too."

*****

It was 7:30 p.m. when Nayana pulled up at Jamila's house. She called her to let her know she was outside. When Jamila walked out the door Nayana said, "Damn mami, you look sexy as hell. I didn't know that dress hugged you like that."

Jamila had on an all-white dress with two slits up her thigh all the way to the bottom of her butt. Her back was cut out with diamonds going down her side. And her chest cut out showing just a little bit of cleavage. She had a French manicure, and her hair was curled down to her shoulders covering the right side of her face. Her skin was a shade darker than yellow and her eyes were light brown. She had on open toe red bottom stilettos with three-inch heels. Jamila was a true queen tonight and she knew it.

Nayana had on an all-black dress with the stomach cut out, so it showed off her six pack. Her back was cut out as well. She had on a platinum dog chain and her hair was pressed down. She was wearing all black stilettos. She was the new Shakira in the flash.

As they pulled up to Jelani's, Jamila said, "Nayana, is that Cordial outside?"

"I think it is him Jamila," replied Nayana.

Cordial had on a dark blue tailored suit on. They could tell he was well built underneath it.

"Nayana, he is too handsome," Jamila said as they walked up to him.

"Hello, Cordial."

"Nayana, I didn't even see you, but you look amazing tonight."

"Thank you. Do you remember my friend Jamila?"

"Yea, it's nice to see you again," said Cordial.

"Likewise," replied Jamila.

"So, ladies shall we go in? Please follow me."

As they went inside, they saw 250 chandeliers with yellow and red crystals in them. Each table had it's on chandelier over it. The painting on the wall looked so real. On the far back wall was a waterfall that went into a small pond.

"Cordial, this place is so beautiful," said Nayana.

"Wait till you see our seats."

"Where are we eating at?" Nayana questioned.

"Over the restaurant in the VIP section. Come on we have to take the elevator to the balcony."

When they reached the top floor, they stepped off the elevator to walk down the hallway. Following the red carpet Nayana touched Jamila's hand and said, "this place is fly girl."

"I know," replied Jamila.

Cordial said, "Our seats are to the right. From here we can see over the whole restaurant, so ladies, do you like it so far?"

Nayana added, "It's amazing in here. I have never seen a place like this before."

"It's so beautiful," said Jamila.

"Fabio will be here in a few minutes. Matter of fact, Jamila if you will look down there, he is walking towards the elevator now. Do you see him?" asked Cordial.

"Yes, I do."

Jamila couldn't take her eyes off him. From the way he carried himself, one could tell he was accustomed to making things happen. He had on an all-black Armani suit with a red tie. She could no longer see him as he stepped on the elevator. Five minutes later he arrived at the table.

"Hello and good evening to all of you. Nayana it's good to see you again."

"You too, Fabio," said Nayana.

"Cordial and Nayana if you don't mind, I would like for me and Jamila to go to our own table," said Fabio.

"No, we don't mind," Cordial said.

"Shall we Jamila?"

"Please after you."

Fabio took her hand as they walked down the hall to a room to the left, Fabio opened the door and said, "This way please."

"Oh my God Fabio. This is beautiful."

"I'm glad you like it. Come look out the window the view is over the whole city. This is where I like to eat when I'm dining here. So how have you been? Tell me a little bit more about yourself." Asked Fabio.

"What would you like to know?" said Jamila.

"How about things that make you smile."

"You know what Fabio. You are good, very good."

"What you mean?" asked Fabio with a smile on his face

"Well Fabio, there's really not much about me. I'm twenty-eight years old. My father was killed by his friend when I was eleven years old. My mother worked two jobs to take care of me. I moved out when I was seventeen years old so my mother and stepfather could have their own space."

"Jamila don't take this the wrong way, but there is so much more to you I see that you're not telling me."

"Fabio, my life is a book, just not an open one. Remember Fabio, always say less than necessary. So, what about you?" asked Jamila.

"How about we order our food up, then I'll tell you about myself." said Fabio.

"That's fine with me."

"What would you like to eat?" asked Fabio.

"How about you order for me?"

"I can do that," Fabio said.

Fabio picked up the phone and ordered the two specials of the day and a bottle of champagne.

"So, like yourself my mother and father were killed when I was eighteen years old and I am an only child. I'm thirty-two years old. My father started up a restaurant in the early 70's and now I'm the owner of it. Other than business I really stay to myself. Look, here is our food coming through the door."

Chapter Seven

"So Nayana would you like to order?" asked Cordial.

"I don't know. Do they have seafood here?"

"Matter fact that's one of the specials of the day. Order me the same thing Nayana," said Cordial.

"How do I get in touch with the waiter? They are so far away." asked Nayana.

"There's a phone on the wall next to you. Pick it up and the waiter will answer it," said Cordial.

"I am so embarrassed. I didn't know that."

"Don't be. I was the same way when I first ate here. Nayana, what would you like to drink?" asked Cordial.

"Red wine," said Nayana.

They talked all night until it was 11:30p.m. They didn't know the restaurant was about to close.

*****

"Jamila, I had a wonderful time with you tonight. Can we do this again?"

"I would like that very much Fabio. How about you call me tomorrow night?" asked Jamila

"I will, beautiful," said Fabio. "Shall we return to our friends.?"

When they got to the table Fabio said, "How did you enjoy yourself this evening?"

Nayana said, "I had a great time with Cordial this evening. What about you?"

"Your friend Jamila is amazing. I enjoyed myself very much."

As Fabio and Cordial walked them to the front door, they said their goodbyes and parted ways.

SAYNOMORE

Chapter Eight

It was 9 am when Jamila called Nayana. She picked up the phone with a harsh, "Hello."

"Wake up beautiful," said Jamila.

"I'm still sleeping. What time is it anyway?"

"9 a.m." said Jamila.

"Why you up so early?" asked Nayana.

"You know I don't sleep late. Plus, I'm on my way over. So, get up, I'll be there in twenty minutes."

"Ugghhh, ok," replied Nayana.

Nayana only lived ten minutes away from Jamila. Jamila walked down her stairs to her car. She looked at her 2006 Lexus. It was white with 17" rims. She got in her car and played 50 Cent's *Best Friend*. When she pulled up at Nayana's house, Nayana was standing in the doorway looking at Jamila with a Guess du-rag on. She had her hand on her hip when Jamila opened her car door. Nayana looked at her, rolled her eyes and walked back to her bedroom. Jamila let out a laugh as she looked at Nayana laying in the bed.

"Nayana get out of bed," said Jamila.

"No, Jamila, it's too early. It's not even 10:00 yet."

Jamila sat next to Nayana and pushed her and said wake up.

"Ok, ok I'm up DAMN," replied Nayana. "So where did Mr. Fabio take you last night since you want to talk?"

"If you must know, Nayana," said Jamila, "I have never seen a place like it in my whole life."

"So, tell me about this place Mami."

"So, after we left the table, we went down the hallway to the left to a room about half the size of the restaurant. The carpet was purple and with black rings on it. There were big and little circles on it as well. The waterfall we saw downstairs, runs from upstairs. Three different waterfalls come together to make a little river that falls downstairs. There are two big glass doors that open up to a beautiful view of the city, with a glass table outside to eat at. Nayana, there's a big glass window in front of it. There is a homemade rainforest with every type of exotic bird you can think of in the middle of the floor. There's a big glass table in the shape of a diamond. The table is also black and purple with little circles on it. On the right wall is a 72" flat screen TV that has a camera on it with a view of the ocean twenty-four hours a day. There are two bars and a jacuzzi that can fit up to twenty-five people. It was so nice," said Jamila."

"Jamila, are you for real?" Nayana asked.

She looked at Nayana and said, "I am girl. my pussy getting wet just by thinking of all that."

"You ain't try to give him the cake?" asked Nayana.

"No, I ain't a fast ass. So how was your time with Cordial's sexy ass? "asked Jamila.

"You can say sexy ass again. We had a good time."

"Did you know there was a phone on the wall, and you had to pick up to get a waitress?" said Nayana. "But he was cool. We had a good time with each other."

Nayana looked at her phone ringing playing the ringtone *Hot Boys* by Missy Elliot. She started smiling to herself. "Let me guess," asked Jamila. "That has to be Cordial."

"Why you want to know?" said Nayana. "But if you must know. yes, it is. Now let me answer the phone please, sheesh. Hello."

"Good morning beautiful. How did you sleep last night?" asked Cordial.

I slept well last night. Why are you up so early?" asked Nayana.

"Because I had to make some runs in the Bronx, around your way," said Cordial. "I was thinking about you and was wondering if you wanted some coffee. I'll bring you one."

"So, you trying to stop by this morning?" asked Nayana, looking at Jamila with a big smile on her face.

"Yea, I am. So how do you like your coffee?" asked Cordial.

"With two sugars and cream," replied Nayana with a little sexiness to her voice.

"Ok, I'll be there in thirty minutes love."

"I'll be waiting," said Nayana.

She hung the phone up and jumped up and said to Jamila, "You have to go. I have to get ready for my company."

Jamila looked at Nayana and said, "Are you kicking me out for some dick?"

"No, I'm kicking you out for a long thick fat dick so yes in so many words," said Nayana.

"Don't call me no more today." Jamila said walking out the door. Sitting in her car she pulled her phone out and texted Fabio.

"Hello Fabio, how are you doing today? I enjoyed my night with you last night. If you are not too busy, I was hoping you would join me today at sunset Park for a little picnic. Just the two of us. If yes, how does 3:30 p.m. sound? Please reply back. Jamila."

Fabio's phone went off with the text from Jamila. As Fabio read his text, he smiled to himself and replied. "Thank you for the invite, and yes I would love that. Do I need to bring anything?"

Jamila replied back, "No just yourself."

After reading the text Jamila drove off.

SAYNOMORE

Chapter Nine

After taking a quick shower, Nayana sprayed her Chanel perfume over her wet body. She then put a pair of boy shorts on so her camel toe would show and then a white beater on so her perfect C cups and big nipples would show pressed tight against her skin. Her caramel skin was so smooth she put on a light coat of lip gloss to her beautiful lips to give them a shine.

She looked out her door to see Cordial pulling up. She waved to him and left her front door open for him.

After walking through Nayana's front door, Cordial heard Sean Paul's *I'm Still In Love With You* playing in the background. He saw Nayana walking from the back room looking sexy as hell. She walked up to him and gave him a kiss on the cheek and one on the lips.

"Damn, you look sexy this morning, beautiful. Let me find out you trying to keep me here," said Cordial.

"That was part of the plan," Nayana said.

"Here's your coffee."

"Thank you."

Nayana put their cups down on the kitchen table and grabbed his hand and led him to the bedroom. She then pushed him down on the bed, dropped to her knees and looked up at him. Licking her lips, she went to unbutton his pants and felt his Glock 45. He looked down at her as she pulled his pants and boxers down to see his thick dick looked to be at least twelve inches hard. She guessed he was eight inches when he was soft. She grabbed it then put it in her mouth. Cordial let out a light moan as she sucked and licked all over his dick and balls. He was as hard as ever. She looked up at him and he grabbed her by the neck and picked her up. She was so wet from sucking his dick. He laid her down on the bed and pulled her boy shorts off and placed his face between her legs and started licking on her pussy. She wrapped her legs around his head and started moaning louder as her hands were rubbing his head. His tongue was moving in circles around her clit. He started biting on her thighs and licking around her pussy lips kissing all the way down her legs.

Cordial stood up and took his shirt off showing his six pack and chest. He picked up her left leg and placed it on his shoulder pulling her to the edge of the bed. Sliding inside her, she let out a loud moan as his dick was ripping her tight pussy open. He gave her long deep strokes as he bit on her neck. She was digging her nails in his back saying "Baby, I can't take this dick," as she started creaming all over it. He pulled out and told her to bend over. She looked up at him and bent over on all fours. Cordial slid in her wet pussy and grabbed her waist and was grinding deep inside her. Her pussy walls felt like they were going to break. As she grabbed the bedcovers, he told her he was cumming. He slid out of her and she dropped to her knees and put his dick in her mouth. Cordial grabbed her head and let out a loud moan as he let his load go in her mouth. He fell back on the bed out of breath. She climbed in the bed next to him and laid her head on his chest. He wrapped his arm around her and kissed her on the forehead. She looked up at him and asked, "You staying with me today?"

"I'm not going nowhere today, beautiful," replied Cordial.

"Good, I'll go make us breakfast."

"Go do that queen."

Chapter Ten

Fabio pulled up at the park and was watching Jamila. She had on a pair of faded blue jeans with rips in them and a light blue shirt that hugged her body and white sandals on. Her hair was pulled back in a ponytail. Fabio got out of his car and walked up to her and gave her a hug.

"So, did you have a hard time finding the park?" asked Jamila.

"No, I didn't, and this food looks good." said Fabio

"I'm glad you think so. Shall we eat?"

With a smile on his face, he nodded. Taking a seat on the bench, Fabio said, "I haven't been on a picnic in years.

Jamila sat across from him and said, "Well I hope you enjoy yourself."

"I know I will. So, tell me what your plans in life are?" asked Fabio.

"While I went to school for business management, I also majored in social skills. You already know I'm a counselor and I think I want to open my own business. What about you?" asked Jamila.

"Let's just say I do my part in my family business," said Fabio.

Jamila looked at him and said, "What's your part?"

"I told you my father started a family business and now it's mine. Over the years, I managed to open up three more restaurants."

"Ok, but what else do you do?" said Jamila with a puzzled look on her face.

Looking at her body language he said, "one day I will tell you I promise. So, tell me have you ever been to Paris?"

Jamila put her finger up as she was eating a bite of her sandwich. She took a sip of lemonade and said, "No I haven't, but I would love to go one day."

"How about you come with me tomorrow for the week. I know we just met but I'm feeling your vibe. And I think you are feeling mine too." said Fabio.

"How do I know you won't kill me or some crazy shit once I get out there?" asked Jamila tilting her head poking her lips out.

"I'm not that type of guy. So, what's up, you coming with me?" said Fabio

"Sure, why not. I'm down. What time we are leaving," asked Jamila.

"Our flight leaves at 8:30 tomorrow morning."

"So, you just knew I was going to come?" Asked Jamila.

"No, I was hoping you would."

"You are too much Fabio, I swear."

"Now I brought two loaves of bread with me to feed the ducks. So, come feed them with me. It will be fun, I promise." said Jamila

"I'm right behind you."

After three hours Jamila was leaving the park when her phone went off.

"Hello beautiful."

"I thought I told you not to call me after you kicked me out today," Jamila said

"Whatever and you would have kicked me out too if you knew what went down with me and Cordial." said Nayana.

"Save me the details. What's up?" asked Jamila

"Elisha's birthday is this week, and he wants us to hang out with him tonight. You, me, Lorenzo and Isaiah."

"Where he wants to go?" asked Jamila

"The Purple Rain, grown and sexy."

"Ok, what time?"

"We are meeting up at his place at 7 p.m."

"Ok, I'll be there. I'll see you then."

Chapter Eleven

"Elisha, I did not know it was like this in here," said Nayana.

"I told you I had a plug to get us in here. You have to know somebody who knows somebody," said Elisha

"I've heard stories about this place, but seeing is believing," Jamila said. It was like every table was VIP and you must dress up to come in here.

"Jamila this is a grown and powerful club. A lot of big hitters come in here. The mayor, judges, DA's, mob bosses. Just look around," Lorenzo told her. You have clouds of smoke in the air from all the smoking. There were people taking shots at the bar wearing $3000 suits. No R&B nor pop music was playing. They were playing soft jazz that Jamila admired. She knew they were going to win by all means. That is why they were in the positions they were in. Sometimes you have to be heartless and get your feet wet.

"Damn, look at all this money in here," said Nayana.

"Elisha, why did you choose this club?" asked Jamila.

"Something different Jamila. Nayana, you swear you are Beyonce, said Elisha.

"Beyonce? Boo boo I'm running neck to neck with her." Nayana said, snapping on Elisha.

"So, you are saying you can get anybody in this club?"

"With no problem," said Nayana.

"Ya hear that right Lorenzo, Isaiah and Jamila.?"

"Why you trying to ride my girl, Elisha?" said Jamila. "My girl knows how to work her ones and twos." Her and Nayana slapped hands over the table and looked at Elisha at the same time.

"Ok, put it to the test then," said Elisha.

"No problem baby boy."

"Let me throw a curveball in it, since you have so much confidence in yourself. You have to get him to go to the VIP private rooms in the back. Tie him up and take a picture for proof," stated Elisha.

"What the fuck you got going on?" Said Jamila.

"Chill Mami, I got this, and I'll do something even better. I'll let you choose the victim," said Nayana with confidence.

"Bet. Give us a few minutes and we will let you know who."

"Come on Nayana," Jamila said. "Let's go get a drink from the bar."

As they walked off Jamila said, "you don't have to do this."

"I can't stand his ass I swear, but I'll show him."

"Hey, can we have two blue muthafuckers," said Jamila.

"So, you see the guy who got three phones over there in the corner by himself?" Elisha gestured.

"Yea, the fat one smoking a cigar?" asked Lorenzo.

"Yea, he's the one."

"Isn't that Tony Lenchee, the crime boss?"

"Yea, that's him Lorenzo."

"You know they not even going to be able to get close to him," said Lorenzo.

"That's the point." Elisha waves them over.

"Come on, Elisha is trying to get our attention, Nayana."

"Who you think it is Jamila?"

As they reached the table, Elisha pointed to the table and said, "the fat man over there smoking."

Nayana started walking over there and Jamila said, "Hey hold up. I'm coming with you."

As they reached the table, two bodyguards stopped them. "What can I do for you?"

Nayana looked at Tony and said, "I want to have a drink with him."

"If you want a drink, what does she want?" asked one of the bodyguards.

"The same thing."

"Do you mind a pat down?" Tony said.

Jamila looked at them and said, "No we do not."

They looked in their Gucci bags and patted them both down. Then they walked past the bodyguards to sit next to Tony.

"They got past the guards," Isaiah said.

Lorenzo just watched.

"What would you like to drink ladies?" asked Tony

"I'll take a bloody Mary," Nayana said.

"And what about you?" asked Tony

"A mind eraser."

One guard walked off to get the drinks. "So, what brings you two here tonight?"

"We just needed to get out tonight and relax no worries. What about you?", Nayana asked.

"I own this club. That's why I'm here."

"That's why you had those bodyguards pat us down?' Jamila said.

"Because of who I am they had too."

"So, what you think they are talking about?" Asked Elisha.

"I don't know but they've been over there almost a half hour now. Tony just been taking shot after shot," replied Lorenzo.

"So, ladies, how about we go to the back. I have a private room back there." asked Tony.

"Ok," said Nayana, rubbing his stomach with her hand.

"Hold on one second," said Tony. "Joey, Joey I'm taking my new friends to the back and I do not want to be disturbed."

"Do you want me to come with you?" asked Joey.

"What part of I don't want to be disturbed don't you understand?" said Tony

"Sorry boss."

"This way ladies."

When they reached the back room, Nayana started licking the side of his face and rubbing his manhood while Jamila watched them.

"Are you going to join us," Tony said to her.

Nayana whispered in his ear, "Have a seat papi," as Tony sat down.

Jamila started taking off her clothes as Tony watched her. He started pulling down his pants.

"Papi, let me cover up your eyes, it will be fun," said Nayana. "Then you can try and guess which one of us is licking on you."

Tony looked at her. "I don't know if it's all the shots I took tonight, or the sexiness I see in front of me but ok. Come on."

Nayana started kissing Tony's stomach and sucking on his nipple as she unbuttoned his shirt. She kissed on Tony long and hard as Jamila covered his eyes up. He put his hands behind his back and Jamila tied them together. Tony was so into what Nayana was doing, he didn't realize what Jamila was doing. Jamila took three pictures of Tony that way with his dick hanging out.

"What's going on?" said Tony. As he went to stand up, he tripped over his pants and hit his head on the coffee table knocking him out cold.

"Nayana shit, we need to go now. I hope no one heard him fall. Come on."

They got dressed and walked out the backroom back to the table and said, "We need to go now."

Lorenzo asked, "Is everything okay?" as he took a sip of his drink.

"Yes, Jamila said, Now come on. I'll meet you outside. Let me thank the security for letting us in. I'll be right out in five minutes." Elisha said.

"Hurry up", said Jamila.

Fifteen minutes later they all were in Lorenzo's truck leaving.

Chapter Twelve

"What the fuck happened? How did Tony get killed in his own fucking club? And by who?" Asked Sammy.

"Nobody knows."

Sammy looked at everyone and said, "All the fuck we know is that he was tied up with his dick out. And rumor has it that his throat slit from ear to fucking ear and nobody knows shit? I want every fucking bodyguard that was here last night right here, right fucking now. I want to see the tape to see who the fuck he was with."

Sunnie looked at Sammy and said, "there is no tape because there were no cameras here. Tony didn't trust them; he would say the Feds can tap into them."

"What the fuck."

"Alex."

"Yeah boss."

"Get some guys down here to clean this place the fuck up and report this to the police. Fuck, Fuck, Fuck me! Have everyone at my house within the hour."

Sunnie said, "y'all heard him. Get this place cleaned and the police down here."

"Alex, take care of this."

"I'm on it. "

Sunnie looked at Sammy and said, "Can I have a word?" Sammy turned around and looked at him.

"Yea, what's on your mind?"

"We are all mad as hell right now. Tony was our brother. I think right now we need to look at other families. Don't forget Tony had two attempts on his life already. He knew that he was a mark and acted like he didn't care."

"Sunnie, I know this, but when you have ten armed men with you, there should be no fucking reason why you get your throat cut from ear to ear. So, all that tells me is it was an inside job. Where were all the bodyguards at when all this happened?" asked Sammy.

"You think Fabio had his hands in this?" asked Sunnie as he watched Sammy walk back and forth across the floor with his hands rubbing his head.

"I don't know, but I want everyone dead who is connected to Fabio. Cordial, that Spanish spick and that nigga Tesfar. Tony will not die alone," Sammy said. He looked at Alex and said, "Pour me a shot of gin. Make it a double shot."

"Sammy, I think you should at least try and have a sit down with him first. Now that Tony's dead, he might have a change of heart knowing his head of protection is gone. Let's send him a message. Have Cordial killed and send him his head," said Sammy.

"And when do you want this done?" asked Sunnie.

"You know we do have the mayor election coming up in the next few days." Sunnie said looking at Sammy taking his shot of gin.

"Tony is dead. Our family is a family that is feared in all of New York and New Jersey. We can't let this go unanswered. We need to answer for this now," said Sammy.

Sammy took a seat and said, "After Tony's funeral service we take back Queens from Fabio."

"And when you plan on having his service?"

"Next week at the Townhall and we will have him laid to rest on Albany avenue. Send word to all the families so they can pay their respects."

"I will."

Chapter Thirteen

It was 1 a.m when Jamila made it home. She took a hot shower and got dressed. It was 3 a.m. when she got in her car. She couldn't stop thinking about what happened. She couldn't believe what they did last night. She knew they were dead if someone caught them. She called Nayana and after two rings, she picked up.

"Hello."

"Hey, listen, I'm leaving for the week." said Jamila

"Where are you going?" asked Nayana

"To Paris for the week with Fabio."

"Are you for real Mami?"

"Yes, I am. I want you to keep an eye on my place while I gone."

"You know I got you, Mami," replied Nayana

"Ok, I left a key under your flowerpot," said Jamila.

"When did you do that?" asked Nayana

"This morning, when I was knocking at your door for twenty minutes and you ain't answer the door."

"I'm sorry, I ain't go to bed until very late."

"Why were you up so late?" asked Jamila. "We dropped you off at midnight."

"I know as soon as y'all pulled off, Cordial pulled up and stayed the night with me. He's still in the bed sleeping."

"You really like him?" asked Jamila

"I do Mami." said Nayana.

"Well, I got to get some errands done before I leave this morning. So, I will talk to you later girl."

"Bye, have fun."

I will try. Don't get pregnant while I'm gone," stated Jamila.

"Okay, Bye Jamila."

"Bye beautiful."

Jamila looked and saw it was 7:20 a.m. She pulled her phone out and called Fabio.

"I'm sorry, I had to make some runs this morning," said Jamila. "What time do you want to meet this morning?"

"How about now?" said Fabio. "Where are you?"

"Driving, I just left my house."

"Okay, meet me at the airport."

"I'll be there in twenty-five minutes. I'm on my way now," said Jamila.

"And you don't have to bring anything with you," said Fabio.

"Hun, so what am I going to wear?" Asked Jamila.

"We will take care of that when we get there," said Fabio.

"Fine with me, I will see you in a few minutes then."

Jamila called Nayana back to let her know she was leaving now.

"Hey, just calling you to let you know I'm leaving. I'll see you when I get back beautiful." said Jamila

"Don't forget me when you go gift shopping," said Nayana.

"I won't. Bye."

Jamila pulled up at the airport and called Fabio to let him know she's outside.

"Ok, I'm waiting on you. Come to the back to gate thirty-two. There is a pass waiting on you."

"I'm on my way," said Jamila.

"The stewardess will lead you to the plane," said Fabio.

"I see gate thirty-two now. I'll see you in a few."

"Hello, is this gate thirty-two, right?" Asked Jamila.

"Yes, it is, how may I help you?"

"Yes, Fabio LaCross told me there is a pass waiting on me here."

"Yes, there is. Are you Jamila?" asked the stewardess.

"I am."

"Can I see your ID please?"

"Sure, here you go," said Jamila

"Thank you and can you follow me please."

Fabio saw Jamila coming and went and gave her a hug.

"It's nice to see you again," said Fabio.

"Likewise. Are we the only ones on this plane besides the pilots and stewardess?" asked Jamila.

"We are. Let's just say I'm treating you like the queen I know you are," said Fabio.

"Fabio, you did not have to do this. It must've cost a fortune," said Jamila

"Don't worry about that. Let's just take our seats so the plane can take off."

Jamila looked at Fabio and held his hand. She leaned in and kissed him on the lips.

SAYNOMORE

Chapter Fourteen

Cordial was rolling up his dutch at the kitchen table getting ready to meet up with Tesfar. He had seven kilos that he had to drop-off in east New York. He hated going down there. Them niggas was hot down there and didn't know how to move. But Dapp's trap was moving three kilos a week plus he had some workers in Maryland that came up for two birds a week.

Fabio sold kilos for $25,000, but if they had to make the drop, it was $7,000 on top of the $25,000. Dapp knew the rules and respected them. How Cordial looked at it was, it was $41,000 on top of $150,000. He already had the seven bricks in the duffle bag on the floor. He went to light his blunt, took a long pull and looked at the blunt then let out a light cough. He grabbed his car keys off the table and duffle bag off the floor. He was heading out the door when he overheard the newscaster saying Tony Lenchee was killed last night. Cordial put everything down and walked back to the living room to catch the news of what happened last night.

"The body of mobster Tony Lenchee was found last night around midnight with his throat slit from ear to ear at his club Purple Rain off of 45 street. Two bodyguards found him tied to a chair. There has been two assassination attempts on his life already, both times failed. Tony Lenchee was best known as The Boss of Bosses or The Untouchable Don. There are no witnesses at this time. As you can see behind me, the club is taped off as detectives investigate the crime scene."

Cordial said, "Damn, low key bodied in his own night club. That had to be an inside job."

He pulled out his phone and texted Fabio who left for Paris early this morning. After he texted Fabio he walked and picked up his blunt out the ashtray and duffle bag off the floor. After he grabbed his car keys to his black-on-black BMW, he walked out the door. He threw the duffle bag in the backseat, got in and drove off.

SAYNOMORE

Chapter Fifteen

"Sammy everyone is here," Alex said to him as he was sitting behind the desk looking out the window.

"Have everyone go to the basement. I'll be down there in a minute."

"Yes sir," said Alex.

Sammy got up and walked out the room downstairs to the basement. As he entered through the door, all eyes were on him. He looked around and said, "I have one question. Where the fuck were you all when Tony got killed?" Ten guys lined the back wall as Sammy pointed his gun at them.

"Who wants to talk first?" asked Sammy. "Don't everyone speak at once. I have a list here with everyone's name on it," Sammy showed them. "It's a count of three hundred guests' names at the door. But what I don't understand is if it's a count of three hundred guests' names at the door, why does the clicker count show three hundred and five people? So here is our mystery. Who are our five ghosts that were here last night that we did not see? Now this is what I want to know. Who was working the front door and who was working the clicker?"

Sammy pointed the gun at Vincent and said, "Don't you work the front door?"

"Yes sir."

"And Nick, weren't you the one clicking as they went in?"

"Yes sir."

"Good now we are getting somewhere. Now let's see. Who was watching over Tony?" Sammy put the top of the gun to his head and said, "If I had to guess, I would say Joey. Was it you?"

"Yes sir."

"And who else? Mark? Everyone but Joey, Mark, Vincent and Nick leave us."

Sammy took off his jacket and laid it on the back of the chair he was behind.

Looking at Vincent he said, "Who were our five-ghost last night? You were marking the names off the list last night, right?"

"Yes."

"So, you let five people pass you?"

Vincent looked down at the floor and said, "No".

"So, why did Nick have three hundred and five guests on his clicker? Wait I know he just clicked five more times out of fun. That's what you are telling me?" said Sammy.

Nick looked at Vincent knowing he was a dead man not saying a word.

"No, he did his job."

Sammy walked up to him and patted him on his back and said, "I'm glad you admitted to that. Nick you can go as well."

Nick looked at Vincent knowing he was dead as soon as he walked past them going upstairs. Sammy walked to the pool table and picked up a pool stick and walked back to his seat and said, "Vincent, I'm not going to toy with you. You can die the easy way or a painful way. It's up to you. But one thing I can promise. You are going to die today. Now how, is your choice."

Vincent looked at Sammy and Alex and said, "it was an old friend of mine's son that I let in. There were five of them. Two girls and three guys, but they're not killers."

"How do you know that? Were you with them all night? I want names and addresses now.

"Scotty McGee is the only one I know. 1405 Simpson Rd. Amityville, New York."

"What do these so-called killers look like?" asked Sammy.

"One of them was black and the other female was Spanish." Joey cut them off.

"Wait, did they have on black and red dresses?"

"Yea, they did." said, Vincent

Sammy looked at Joey and said, "Wait you saw them?"

"Yea, I patted them down. They were with Tony last night. He took them to the back room."

Sammy looked at Vincent and swung the pool stick, smacking him in the face, knocking him to the ground, Sammy yelled, "They not killers." As he kicked him in the face over and over again. He pulled his gun out and shot Vincent eight times in the face and chest.

Joey started speaking fast, "I swear I ain't know. Tony told us to leave him alone and to go back to the front. So, we did. You know how he was."

Sammy said out of breath, "I know how he was, and I know you're telling the truth. So, what you and Mark are going to do is go by Scotty's house and pay him a visit. I want everybody there dead. *Everything* dead. And Joey, if you and Mark mess this up, I swear you two will wish you were dead when I'm done with you. Now get rid of this body and go to work. Alex, find out who our girls are. I have some affairs to deal with now. We will talk later," said Sammy looking at Vincent's dead body one more time before leaving.

SAYNOMORE

Chapter Sixteen

Cordial pulled up at the 40's project in Queens. Tesfar was smoking a blunt and talking with a female when he saw Cordial's car pull up. He told her he had some business to take care of and he pushed off. He opened up the car door and got in.

"What's good, rude boy? Said Tesfar.

"Shit, trying to set up some pussy for later."

"Facts. You ready for the ride?" asked Cordial.

"Good and pass that blunt. That shit smell good as fuck."

"Ya mon, it's that purple hazel," Tesfar said, pulling on it one more time before passing it to Cordial.

"No shit. You know what I wanted to tell you?" Cordial said between puffs of the blunt. "I was watching the news this morning and that boy Tony Lenchee was rolled last night. No bullshit, they said his throat was cut from ear to ear."

"Where at?" asked Tesfar.

"The crazy shit is it happened in his club."

"Blood clot. What the fuck? What Fabio say about this?"

"Fabio don't know yet. He went to Paris this morning with baby girl from the club last week. I texted his phone to let him know but he ain't hit me back yet."

"Who you think rocked him to sleep?" said Tesfar.

"Shit, I don't know, rude boy. There goes that 30% to 40% Tony was talking about."

"So, where are we meeting these niggas at?" Tesfar asked.

"Same spot as always." Cordial replied. "Tesfar, I wanted to ask you where the hell you went last night at the club?"

"My side piece hit my line after twenty minutes of being in the club, so I slid out. Besides you and Fabio were all boo'ed up and shit. So how long he gonna be gone?" Asked Tesfar.

"Shit I think he said a week.:

"Cordial, we really need to tighten up all the way now. That boy Sammy gonna try something. He already doesn't like Fabio," said Tesfar.

"Fuck him. Let him try something. The muthafuckers bleed just like everyone else. And Tony is proof of that. Tesfar you done laid down more niggas down in Queens then anyone."

"It's not about how many niggas I laid down or you," said Tesfar. "All we know is they looking for us right now. Real shit, and we going to east New York. We need to have them meet us somewhere closer. This is really their side of town. This ain't Queens, Harlem or the Bronx," said Tesfar.

"Nigga you sound scared," said Cordial.

"I ain't scared of shit nigga. It's just that, we are riding in a black-on-black BMW and everyone knows whose car this is. We might have a hit on us for some shit we ain't have nothing to do with at all."

"Bro, I feel you. We always had each other's back. Plus, look we already here. That's his trap house right there. So, let's just make this play and get back to Queens." When they pulled up, Cordial grabbed the bag from the backseat and walked to the front door with Tesfar right by his side. The front door opened. "Yoo. What's good? I been waiting on you. Come in."

Cordial dapped him up while Tesfar just looked at his goofy ass. He never did like him. When they walked in the house, Dapp said, "the money is right there, homie. $191,000 cash."

"And there you go, seven of them in the bag." Cordial placed the bag on the table and pulled out the money Dapp had on the table to count it.

As Tesfar watched Dapp dig a knife in the top of the brick of cocaine, pulled it out and sniffed the coke off the tip of it in front of Tesfar, to make sure it was good. Tesfar looked at the house they were in. As much as he didn't like Dapp, he had to say his spot was fly. It didn't look like a trap house at all. He respected that Dapp didn't have a bunch of niggas in there when they pulled up to take care of business.

"Damn, damn, damn. Cordial this shit is Grade A shit," said Dapp.

"Always my guy. Yo, Tes we out. Money's good." Cordial gave Dapp a pound and stepped outside. Tesfar looked at Dapp and gave him a head nod then walked out the door.

*****

Nayana texted Cordial.

"Hey handsome, I was wondering if you were coming by tonight. Just hit me back and let me know," Nayana

Cordial looked at his phone ringing he picked it up and saw Nayana had texted him. He smirked and replied.

"Yea, I will be there around 7 tonight baby girl."

Nayana looked at her phone and smiled. She then saw Isaiah was calling her.

"Hey what's up Isaiah?"

"Shit did you see the news last night?"

"No, what happened?" asked Nayana.

"Tony Lenchee was killed last night."

"Who is that?" Said Nayana.

"The one you and Jamila were with."

"What the fuck? How did he die?" asked Nayana.

"They said someone slit his throat."

"Damn, did you call Lorenzo and Elisha to tell them?"

"Elisha already knows and Lorenzo or Jamila ain't pick up."

"Well Jamila's in Paris with her new friend."

"With whom?" asked Isaiah.

"Some guy she talks too. "

"Whoa, that's crazy."

"You know how Jamila is. She always doing something, but she will be ok. She knows how to handle herself."

"Nayana, remember how she always read *The 48 Law of Power* and *The Art of Law*?

"Isaiah, she studied those books. She read them for years and took notes. I'm about to go shopping Isaiah, so I'll talk with you later." Said Nayana.

"Ok, bye."

Nayana laid back on her head and was thinking how she was just kissing on Tony and didn't know who he was. And now he's dead. She covered her face with her pillow and yelled.

Chapter Seventeen

"Abby let's go out to eat or a movie, something," Elisha said.

"I can't. I have to study for this test tomorrow at work. They got somebody from IP coming down. So, we all have to be on point with IP."

"What's IP?" asked Elisha.

"International Ports." Replied Abby.

Elisha walked in the room and was looking at Abby on her laptop and said, "Baby, we been together for five years now. "

Abby stopped and looked at him.

"Abby, I love you with all my heart plus my soul. You are my everything and I am asking you on one knee will you marry me and be my wife?"

"Oh my God, Elisha yes, yes, yes baby. I will marry you."

She hugged and kissed all over him.

"So tomorrow we will go see my mother and father to tell them the good news. Matter of fact I'm taking off tomorrow. Come on baby. Let's go out to eat," Abby said.

"I thought you had a test and IP was coming to your job tomorrow." Said Elisha.

"Don't worry about that. Just worry about what I'm gonna do to you when we come home tonight baby."

*****

"So, Jamila, how do you like Paris?" asked Fabio.

"It's beautiful. I love it here." Said Jamila.

"I was raised here."

"So, do you still live here?"

"Here and New York. But most of the time here." Jamila walked up to a picture on the wall and looked at it. "I'm guessing this is a picture of your father."

"Yea, that's him." Said Fabio.

"You look just like him."

"If you don't mind me asking, how did he get killed?" asked Jamila.

"Well, I don't mind. Come have a seat next to me over here on the love seat. I never talked about it, but it is about time I do. I really don't know all the details. All I know it was a very old friend of his who tried to get him to clean some money up for him. But he refused. They had four meetings about it, but my father stood his ground. He was an honest businessman and didn't want any part in the crime business. So, he tried to give back the $50,000 and $10,000 on top of that for the loan he was given to open up the restaurant in New York City. But the guy refused to take it back. The last time I saw my father he was going to a meeting. He told me *always stand your ground*. He kissed my forehead and said everything is going to be alright. But I knew it wasn't.

"Later that day my father and mother were leaving the restaurant and a UPS truck pulled up next to their car. Some guys jumped out and let off multiple shots killing them both in cold blood. The police said it was a hit on their life. His friend's name came up several times but when you have judges and DA's in your back pocket, anything goes. So, nothing was able to stick."

"So, what else happened?" Jamila asked him.

"A few weeks later, the same man came and talked to me after I took over the establishment. I told him the same thing my father said to him and that was no. After that I got a few more calls, but I stood my ground and never gave in."

"I'm so sorry to hear that," said Jamila

"It's ok. I'm over it now. Jamila you know why you caught my eye?" asked Fabio. "You remind me of my mother. You favor her a little. Come look."

They walked over to the picture on the wall of his mother.

"See that's her," said Fabio.

"I do. Oh my God. She is so beautiful Fabio."

"Thank you." Fabio's phone went off. He went to pick it up and he saw where Cordial had paged him.

"Shit is crazy, I just saw the news. Tony Lenchee is dead. Someone cut his throat last night from ear to ear. The police don't know who's involved or how it happened. It's all over the news. I saw it on Channel 7 news."

Fabio pulled the news up on his iPhone and was reading the story when Jamila walked up behind him.

"Is everything ok?" asked Jamila

"Yea, how about we go for a ride in the park and get something to eat afterwards? How does that sound?" asked Fabio.

"Wonderful."

SAYNOMORE

Chapter Eighteen

"Is that the house?" Joey said.

"It's the address Vincent gave Sammy," Alex said.

"So, listen, we are going to make this look really clean. Joey you go to the door and say this is Statewide Homecare Insurance. Nick, go with him. When y'all get inside, I will pull up and we will do what we need to do. Get this done as quickly as possible."

*****

"Abby, hurry up. I'm trying to make it to my parents' house sometime this year," Elisha said.

"I'm coming baby. I'm walking down the stairs now."

"Ok, meet me in the car."

"Let me lock up the house and I'll be right out," said Abby.

"Mom. Mom there's someone knocking at the door."

"Oka,y here I come. Now Anthony go upstairs and get ready. Your brother is on the way over."

"Yes mom."

When she opened the door, she saw two men well dressed. One had a briefcase in his hand.

"Hello, how may I help you?" asked Mrs. McGee

"Mrs. McGee?"

"Yes, that's me."

"My name is Joey and I'm with Statewide Homecare Insurance."

"I have home insurance already," she replied.

"Can I show you a few of our plans?" asked Joey. "If you have the time."

"I'm sorry, I don't have the time right now." When she said that Joey hit her with his fist knocking her down to the floor. As she fell, she let out a loud scream. Her husband came running down the stairs calling her name. When he reached the last step, Nick smacked him in the face with his gun knocking him out cold. Jasmine was on the floor holding her head as blood was gushing out.

Alex walked in and said, "Is there anybody else in this house?"

"Leave my mommy alone."

"Anthony run! Run."

As Anthony ran toward the backdoor, Nick shot him dead. Jasmine let out a loud cry.

"Nooo!"

"Kill them and let's get out of here. Joey you set the house on fire."

As Elisha pulled up, he got out of the car.

"Alex, somebody just pulled up. Wait Nick. Ain't that the boy from the club?" asked Joey.

"Yea, that's him. He needs to die too."

As Elisha walked up to the house, he looked back at Abby and said, "Come on."

She yells, "I'm coming now."

When Elisha walked in the house, Joey grabbed him and slammed him on the ground next to his mother. Elisha tried to fight back but Nick smacked him in the face with the gun. His body hit the ground hard. He was dizzy from the blow. Abby walked into the house and screamed. She tried to run back outside but Alex grabbed her and shot her three times in the back and one in the head. Her body dropped right outside the front door.

Elisha saw everything, but it was a blur to him. Still dizzy from the blow to the head, his mother touched his hand and said, "Run," as he looked at his mother with blood on her face and his father laying on the floor knocked out. When Joey looked at Nick, Elisha ran for the back door. Nick shot him two times in the leg and once in the shoulder as he opened the back door and ran out. He went to jump the gate and Joey shot him in the back flipping him over the gate hard. Alex yelled, "get him, make sure he's dead."

"There's no time." Nick said.

"Fuck," Alex said, then he shot Jasmine in the head two times and Scotty two times in the head killing him too.

"Come on. You hear that," said Joey. The police are coming." Alex yelled. "Come on burn the place down. Come on."

As they ran to the van and drove off, the police got there four minutes later, just in time to put the fire out. Elisha lost so much blood, he passed out two streets over. He was found lying face down in the middle of the street by a cop and was rushed to the hospital. Alex called Sammy once they were out of site.

"Sammy everything is done. They put new carpet down and painted the house. But it started to rain, and we had to get out of there."

"Ok, that's good to hear" said Sammy. "That's why I put my trust in you. How long before you get back?"

Twenty-five to thirty minutes," said Alex. "After we burn the van."

"I'll see you then."

SAYNOMORE

Chapter Nineteen

"Breaking news this is Barbara Smith with Channel 7 Eyewitness News. We are on Simpson street where a family was killed, and a victim rushed to the hospital with serious life- threatening injuries. No names have been released yet. The house was set on fire, but the local police were about to put the fire out before the house went into flames. We do know three Caucasian males were here. Wait, I'm getting an update. Now the victims were just identified as forty-two-year-old Jasmine McGee, forty-six-year-old Kevin Mchee, seven-year-old Anthony O'Neal and family friend, twenty-six year old Abby Russ. All the police know is that three Caucasian males were in a white van. If you have any information, please contact the police station or call 1-800 Crime Stoppers. All phone calls are confidential. This is Barbara Smith with Channel 7 Eyewitness News."

*****

"Fabio, Paris is a magical place. I don't ever want to leave here. I've never been on a carriage ride through a park. The people here are nice, and the food is to die for," said Jamila as she was holding his arm.

They walked back to his place feeling the warm breeze of the midnight air.

"I'm glad you like it Jamila," Fabio said. "I'm glad you came with me."

"Me too," Jamila said as she looked up at all the streetlights and how they were lined up on the side of the street. As they reached Fabio's condo, walking up the stairs he opened the door and asked Jamila if she wanted something to drink?"

"Yea, I would like that."

As Fabio was getting their drinks Jamila heard Tevin Campbell's *Can We Talk* playing over the radio.

"Oh my God, Fabio. Come dance with me. That's my song."
Said Jamila as she started moving her body in a sexy way dancing

up to Fabio. She wrapped her hands around his neck and looked at his eyes singing the song to him as she moved her head from side to side. She then kissed him on the lips and her tongue found its way in his mouth.

Fabio started kissing her back. He picked her up and carried her to the bedroom. He laid her down on the bed and started kissing her neck and licking all over it. Jamila leaned up and pulled her shirt off as Fabio's tongue found its way down her stomach and back up to her breast.

Jamila looked at him as he took off his shirt showing his eight pack and chest off to her. She reached for his pants and unbuttoned them as she pulled down his boxers. She looked up at him. His dick was ten inches long and thick. She grabbed it and Fabio moved her hand off his dick and picked her up and laid her down on the bed. He pulled her dress up and started licking and sucking all over her pussy. She moved her hips in a circular motion all over his face. He had both of his arms wrapped around her legs and her hands pushing his head down on her pussy as she let out soft moans. Fabio started sucking on her clit. She tried to wrap her legs around his head, but he wouldn't let her. All she could do was moan louder. She tried to run backwards but he was too strong and wouldn't let her move.

"I'm cumming baby. I cumming," Jamila yelled. "Oh my God baby."

Jamila started shaking as she squirted all in Fabio's mouth. She started fucking his face harder and harder. Fabio's face was wet all over. He looked at Jamila and slid himself inside her. She was so tight, she let out a loud moan. He grabbed her waist with both hands and started stroking long and deep in her wet pussy. Jamila was biting her bottom lip as her hand was gripping the sheets. Fabio let out a loud groan as he started pounding harder and deeper in her. Jamila felt his balls smacking her ass. He pulled out and was watching his dick slide in and out of her wet pussy as she creamed all over it.

Jamila was out of breath. He turned her over on all fours and slid in her doggy style. That's when he heard 50 Cent's *21 Questions* and started fucking her and smacking her ass long dick

68

style. Biting his lips, he wrapped his arm around her waist and pulled her all the way on his dick grinding deep in her pussy. Jamila was screaming, "Baby, baby.". He leaned forward and took his other arm and wrapped it under her titties, grabbing her shoulder with his one leg on the bed.

"I'm cumming baby," he said as he released inside her. His body went limp as he pulled out and laid next to her kissing her on the lips.

She wrapped her arms around him and said, "baby, you didn't give me a chance to take my dress or shoes off," said Jamila.

"Your pussy was too good. Damn." He kissed her forehead, and she kissed his chin.

SAYNOMORE

Chapter Twenty

Fabio and Jamila were laying down when Fabio's phone went off. He reached for it and put it on speaker phone. With his eyes still locked on Jamila's bare body he said, "Hello"

"This is Sammy."

When he heard that, he sat up in the bed. Jamila was looking at him as he talked on the phone. "What can I do for you?" said Fabio.

"By now you heard of Tony's death. So, I'm calling out of respect for him to let you know. The funeral is Monday at the Townhall in Brooklyn at noon and I expect you to be there."

"Well, what if I tell you I can't make it?" says Fabio

"I'm not asking, I'm telling you to be there." After those words Sammy hung up the phone.

Fabio looked at Jamila. She looked back at him.

"I'm sorry, I have to cut our trip short and go back to NY."

"It's okay, I had a great time these few days we been out here," said Jamila.

"I'm glad you said that," said Fabio. "I'll go get us something to eat. I'll be back in a few."

"I'm just going to watch TV and lay here until you get back," said Jamila

"The TV in the den picks up American TV if you didn't know," said Fabio.

"Okay, I'll go watch that TV until you get back." Jamila smiled beautifully as she watched him get dressed and leave.

*****

Nayana heard a loud banging on her door. When she looked out it was Isaiah. She opened her door looking crazy at him.

"Why are you banging on my door like the damn police," Nayana snapped. "Anyway, did you hear from Elisha?"

"No, I haven't heard from him since the night we all went to the club why?" Asked Isaiah

"You are banging on my door and Lorenzo blowing my phone up."

"So why you ain't pick up for him?" asked Isaiah

"I was busy. Let me call him back now. You tripping today. Yea, Lorenzo. When you called, I was away from my phone. What's up?"

"What you mean what's up? Did you see the news last night?" asked Lorenzo.

"No why?" said Nayana. "You talking about Tony's death? I know about that already."

"Fuck him this is about Elisha," said Lorenzo.

"What's wrong with him?" asked Nayana.

"Elisha's whole family is dead, everyone. It happened three days ago. It's all over the news and Abby is dead too, Nayana"

'Oh my God Lorenzo. Are you for real?"

"What's he saying, Nayana?" Isaiah asked her.

"Elisha's whole family is dead and so is Abby. It's all over the news."

"Nayana don't play like that."

"I'm not. Turn to the news," said Nayana

"Fuck, ask him where Elisha is at?" said Isaiah.

"Oh my God, I see the house on the news now. Lorenzo, Oh my God it's true. Where is Elisha at?" Nayana was in a panic.

"He was the one who got shot multiple times. He's in the hospital."

"Lorenzo let me call Jamila. Me and Isaiah are going to the hospital." Said Nayana.

"I'll meet you up there."

"Come on Isaiah. we need to go to the hospital now."

Chapter Twenty-One

"Jamila you see this tree right here?" Said Fabio.

"It looks very old."

"It is. My father told my mother at this very tree twenty years before I was born, he loved her right where we are standing now. Now I'm telling you that I love you and care for you at the very same spot."

Jamila looked at Fabio and said, "I love you too baby."

"So, did you have a good time out here?" asked Fabio.

"I had a great time out here. I enjoyed every moment out here with you. Hold on one second Nayana is calling me."

"Hello, beautiful."

"Jamila listen, Elisha's whole family got killed and so did Abby. Elisha's been shot really bad. I'm on my way to the hospital now to go see him," said Nayana.

"Oh my god when did this happen?" Asked Jamila

"A few days ago. I just found out."

"Nayana tell me this isn't true."

"Jamila it's true. You need to come home now," said Nayana

"I'm leaving today. I'll call you when I get there. Bye."

Fabio looked at Jamila, "Is everything ok?"

"No, my friend's family got killed and he got shot really bad. He's in the hospital. Come on baby. Let's go get our things. We are leaving now to go back to New York."

Fabio held Jamila's hand and said, "There's a lot I want to tell you but not right now. When we get back to New York, we need to sit down and talk."

Jamila just looked at him and shook her head.

*****

"Alex look, ain't that one of Fabio's guys right there with the blue and black shirt on?" Mark asked him.

"Yea, that's that nigga Tesfar."

"You want me to follow him?" said Alex.

"Yea follow him and let me call Sammy to see what he wants done."

Sammy was sitting behind his desk with a few lines of cocaine on it. He took a dollar bill, rolled it up and snorted two lines of coke, then he leaned his head back. His office door was closed, and he had his window open for light. Sammy looked at his phone ringing and picked it up.

"Yea?" said Sammy.

"Hey boss, I see that nigga Tesfar, one of Fabio's guys. Stand down or what?" asked Alex.

"Take the life out of his body. I want him dead to send Fabio a fucking message when you try the Lenacci family."

"Copy Boss."

Sammy looked at the bottle of Jack Daniels sitting on the desk. He poured himself a shot and stood up and said, "For you Tony, I'll kill all them fuckers I swear."

"What he say?" Mark asked.

"He needs to be swimming with the fishes," said Alex

"Let me out. I'll walk up behind him, you drive up. When I'm close enough, I'll let him have it from behind. Two shots to the head and he's dead. Quick and easy. Go ahead and pull over up there," Alex told him.

Alex got out and had his gun in his hand in the fold of his coat walking behind Tesfar.

Tesfar stopped to light his cigarette when he noticed a black town car riding passed him slowly with one Italian in it. He acted like he needed to block the wind to light his cig. So, he stopped by a storefront window to see his reflection behind him. That's when he saw another Italian walking with his hand in the fold of his coat. He knew it was about to go down, so he dropped his CI and pulled his guns out fast and turned around and started shooting at Alex. Alex got shot in the shoulder. You heard people yelling get down and call the police. Screaming was all you heard and people running to get out of the way. Alex went to get up and Tesfar shot him again making him fall backwards to the ground. Tesfar was yelling, "You want to kill me? You have to come better than that fuck boy. Who the fuck want to rump with me blood clot?"

He pointed his guns at Alex's face. That's when you heard the rounds being let off and Tesfar's body being shot up. Mark held a Mac-11 in his hand as Tesfar's body was being ripped apart. He dropped his guns and fell face first on the ground laying in a pool of blood, dead.

Mark picked Alex up and got him in the car and drove off. You had people hiding behind cars watching the whole thing.

SAYNOMORE

Chapter Twenty-Two

Jamila and Fabio walked through the airport. It was 10 p.m. Sunday night when Fabio walked her to her car.

"Jamila, I have some things I need to take care of tomorrow morning. I'll be tied up till about 3:30 maybe 4," said Fabio.

"Ok, call me when you are freed up," said Jamila.

"I will. You go check on your friend."

She kissed Fabio on the lips, and he watched her get in her car and drive off.

Jamila called Nayana, after a few rings she picked the phone.

"Hello," said Nayana.

"Hey, I'm back. Where are you?" said Jamila.

"I'm at home."

"Did you check on Elisha?" Asked Jamila

"Jamila, he's in an induced coma. He got shot four times. Twice in the leg and one in the shoulder and back. He lost a lot of blood. They had to give him a blood transfusion," said Nayana.

"I'm on my way up there to see him now."

"You can't", said Nayana. "He's in ICU and you have to be a family member to see him. I had hell trying to find out what happened. And I still don't have all the details."

"What did Lorenzo have to say?" asked Jamila.

"Nothing really," said Nayana. "Isaiah snapped up there and had to be escorted out."

"I'm about to go home shower and get some sleep. I'll go up there tomorrow morning," replied Jamila.

"Ok, good night."

"Goodnight Nayana."

Jamila drove by Elisha's house and stopped in front of it. She got out of her car and walked up to the front door. You could still see the blood on the concrete. She turned around, got back in her car and drove off. It was 11:30 pm when she walked through her front door. She made a sandwich and laid down on her bed. She didn't understand why Elisha's family got killed and what could they have done for this to happen to them.

*****

"Sammy, we have the FBI outside taking pictures of everybody here."

"That doesn't surprise me at all," said Sammy, looking down at Tony laying in a black coffin with gold handles on it. He was dressed in an all-white suit with a black tie. He had every type of flower surrounding him. And pictures of him smiling with family and friends.

"Sunnie this man was my brother, my brother. Now he's dead," said Sammy wiping a tear from his eye.

"Have you seen Fabio yet?" asked Sammy.

"No, why do you care if he comes or not?"

"Because now that Tony is gone, he will give me what I want, or he will end up like Tesfar. And I will have that establishment burned down to the ground."

"Sammy, we have so many other businesses we can wash our money through," said Sunnie.

"I know this, but I don't like how he feels he can turn the Lenacci family down. Look around Sunnie. What do you see?" Said Sammy. "The Gambino family, the Gotti family, Scott family, Landon family and Denior family are all here paying their respects. And where the fuck is he at? He would have been dead if it was up to me. Tony spared his life because that was his God son. He didn't spare his mother and father. I remember that day Sammy," said Sunnie.

"Sunnie, make sure everybody is in the right seat and Fabio's seat isn't taken," said Sammy.

"Sure, thing Sammy."

Chapter Twenty-Three

Fabio pulled up and looked at all the cars that were there as he walked to the front door.

"Detective Morris, look, isn't that Fabio LaCross?"

"Yes, it is."

"What is he doing at a Mobster's funeral?"

"Showing his respects or he could be glad the man who killed his family is dead now. To just see for himself."

"When the doors opened up, all eyes were on Fabio as he walked towards Tony's casket and looked down at him. Then he took his seat next to Sammy."

"You are late," Sammy said.

"I'm here. That's all that matters."

"We need to talk, Fabio." said Sammy.

"About what?"

"Not here. How about you come to the house when all this is done?" Said Sammy.

"I have some things to take care of," said Fabio.

"Tomorrow then?"

"I'll see." Fabio looked at Sammy and said in his ear. "The answer is still no."

He went to walk out Sammy asked him, "Where are you going?"

"I showed my respects now I'm leaving Sammy." Fabio walked off shaking his head with a smile on his face. He pushed open the doors and looked up at the sky as he walked off.

"I guess you were right, Detective Morris. He did just want to see the man who had his mother and father killed."

"Come on. Let's meet him at his car. You remember the shooting yesterday?" Asked Detective Morris

"Yes, Tesfar King."

"That was one of Fabio's guys believe it or not." When Fabio turned around Detective Morris said, "Sorry for your loss Mr. LaCross."

Fabio looked at him and said, "Why? I'm happy the fat son of a bitch is dead."

Detective Morris said, "I can give two fucks about Tony Lenacci." He leaned on Fabio's car and said, "I'm talking about Tesfar King."

Fabio looked puzzled.

"You didn't know?" Said Detective Morris "Well yesterday he was gunned down bad right off 125th in front of the pizza shop. He took I think the report said thirty-five to forty rounds."

Fabio looked at him and said, "What's your name Detective?"

"I'm Detective Morris and this is Detective Carter."

Fabio looked at him and said, "Well Detectives, you two have a nice day."

Fabio hit the alarm to his car, got in and drove away. He pulled his phone out and called Tesfar's phone three times back-to-back. When he didn't pick up, he stopped at the pizza shop and saw all the dried-up blood in the front. He walked in and said, "I would like a large pizza with the works."

"Coming right up," said the pizza man. "That will be $13.30."

Fabio dropped five $100 bills on the counter and "What happened here yesterday?"

The pizza man looked both ways and said, "I don't want no trouble bro."

"He was my friend," Fabio said.

"Look, all I saw was one white dude. He shot him and was standing over him about to shoot him again when someone else came from the back and shot him up. He didn't even see it coming."

Fabio looked at him and said, thank you, grabbed his pizza and left. He knew then Sammy was behind this. He called Cordial and told him to meet him at the restaurant. Fabio knew Sammy was going to try something. He just didn't know it was going to be this fast. He knew if he didn't put him six feet down, he was dead real soon. Parking his car, he walked right in Jelani and right to the elevator with his pizza in his hand. Cordial was there in twenty minutes.

"What's the word? How was the trip?" asked Cordial.

Fabio looked at him and said, "That's what the fuck you have to ask me? How the fuck was my trip?" said Fabio. Won't you ask me how the fuck Tesfar got killed yesterday and by who?"

"What are you talking about? Tesfar ain't dead." Cordial was confused.

"Yes, the fuck he is. How the fuck you didn't know this, but I do? You know why because you always chasing pussy nigga." Said Fabio.

"You just took some pussy on a trip."

Fabio looked at him and said, "have someone claim his body make sure everything is paid for. The funeral and all. We take care of ours. Dead or alive."

"Fabio my bad man. I really didn't know." said Cordial.

Fabio didn't say a word, he just walked off.

Cordial looked at him. Then went and did what Fabio told him to do.

SAYNOMORE

Chapter Twenty-Four

Fabio walked out of the restaurant and called Jamila.
"Hello," she answered.
"Hey, where you at?" said Fabio.
"I just left the hospital," said Jamila.
"How is your friend?"
"He's in a coma. He lost a lot of blood but he's going to be good."
"If you ain't busy I want you to come with me somewhere," asked Fabio.
"Where you want me to meet you at?" said Jamila
"Come to Jelani."
"I'm on my way now." Said Jamila.
"I'll be out front waiting on you."
Seeing Jamila walking up, Fabio gave her a hug and kiss then walked her to his car.
"Where are we going?" asked Jamila.
"To a friend of mine's house," said Fabio.
As Fabio pulled up to a big white gate, Jamila looked at him and the gates. She knew then what he wanted to talk to her about. The gate opened up and the driveway was five minutes from the house with trees lined up on both sides. When they pulled up to the house, you had men walking around with guns and dogs. They opened the door and got out. Fabio looked at Frankie and helped Jamila out the car. Frankie walked down the stairs and greeted them both and said, "come inside." They walked in the house Frankie said, "Fabio, it's been a long time. When I saw you today, I was very surprised to see you at the funeral."
"I was just showing my respects for the dead. Frankie, this is Jamila. Jamila this is Frankie. He is like a father to me."
Frankie looked at Jamila and said, "you must mean a lot to him for him to bring you to meet me. So, Fabio what brings you by?"
"Sammy wants me to meet him at 3 pm tomorrow at the house."
"I knew this was going to happen. If you go there, you are a dead man." Said Frankie. "You do know this Fabio? I suggest you

meet him at a place you chose on your grounds. So, do you know who killed Tony?" asked Fabio.

"Nobody knows."

"Word is he was last seen with a black and Spanish girl at his club. Sammy's out for blood. He had a family wiped out already behind who he thinks had something to do with it," said Fabio.

"They did what two families couldn't do. Fabio, I don't want nothing to happen to you." Jamila just sat there listening to everything that was said not saying a word. Frankie watched her and was very impressed because she was acting like she wasn't paying them no attention. But he knew she was. What caught his eye is when she picked up the newspaper and was looking at the picture of Tony Lenacci on the cover. He knew then that there was much more to Jamila than what Fabio knew. From the look on her face, when she saw his picture he wondered if she could be a killer that nobody knew.

"Excuse me Fabio for a second. Jamila, have you seen that man on the cover of the paper before?"

"Yes, I have." said Jamila. "Why you ask me that?"

"Because the way you looked at him when you saw his face on the paper." Said Frankie.

"Who doesn't know Tony Lenacci? After all he was a mobster. How the paper says it: *The Boss of Bosses*. The Untouchable Don," Jamila said with a smirk.

"So, Fabio, where did you meet Jamila at?" asked Frankie

"Boy Boy's a few weeks ago and she has been a blessing ever since then."

Jamila knew Frankie wanted to know more about her. As they left Frankie said to Jamila you are welcome here anytime.

"Thank you." said Jamila with a smile.

"Jamila, there's something about you Frankie likes. I have never heard him tell anybody he just met that. I wanted you to meet Frankie. He showed me how to make a living for myself.

Jamila cut him off. "I know what you do already. I'm not dumb. I've been put two and two together and meeting Frankie was just icing on the cake."

At that time Fabio's phone went off.

"Hold on bae. Yea."

"What time are we meeting tomorrow?" asked Sammy

"There's no point for us to meet up. Tony is dead so delete my number."

Fabio hung up the phone and looked at Jamila and said, "I'll drop you off to your car. Come to the restaurant tomorrow around 1 pm."

"Ok, I will be there."

SAYNOMORE

Chapter Twenty-Five

Sammy looked at his phone and said, "Tomorrow we are going to Jelani's. The five of us are going to end this bullshit with Fabio once and for all. That disrespectful pig. If we weren't at Tony's funeral and the FBI wasn't out there, I would have killed his ass. Sunnie, you, Alex, Joey, Mark and myself. Let them know."

"Sure, thing boss," said Sunnie.

"You know Alex is still a little sore from the shots he took a few days ago."

Sammy looked at him and pulled his cigar. "You're right. Get Bull. I'll take care of that now."

*****

Nayana was lying on Cordial's chest rubbing his hands. "Baby, what's wrong? You've been quiet all day." Nayana asked him.

He looked at her and said, "What is loyalty really worth in the end? A picture on a shirt and a shot of liquor for the dead? Pride is what kills niggas," said Cordial.

"Where is all this coming from?" said Nayana

"Fabio and I had a fall out today."

"For what?" Asked Nayana.

"You remember the Jamaican with the long locs that was in VIP with us? He was only there for a few minutes with us."

"Yea, I remember him," said Nayana

"He got killed yesterday because of Fabio's pride. All we did was give his mother $80,000 and paid for his funeral. If Fabio would have just given Tony the $60,000, he would be still here with us."

Nayana took her hand and put it on his chin and pulled his face towards hers and said, "What you mean Fabio's pride? Ask yourself this Cordial, whose life means more to you, yours or Fabio's? His pride got one of you killed already. Let me put it to you this way. Muthafuckers go to jail for life because they didn't snitch on anyone. While he is doing hard time, they homies are smoking, partying and fucking. Yea, they might send him a food package or clothing package the first few years, but after that it stops. Just like when muthafuckers get killed, you talk about them the first year and after that, life goes on. You know what kills me about people? They always talking about loyalty but ask yourself this, how strong is Fabio's loyalty to you?" said Nayana.

"You know what, you are right," said Cordial. "I need to go see Sammy tomorrow morning at the diner and let him know that I'm breaking all ties with Fabio. Matter of fact, I'll take care of that business now."

Nayana put her hand on his chest and said, "No, you have some other business to take care of now." She leaned up and pulled down his boxers and started sucking his dick, rubbing his balls at the same time. Cordial closed his eyes and said, "yea, I'll go do that tomorrow," as Nayana was deep throating him making slurping noises. He grabbed her head and started fucking her mouth. "Damn baby, I'm about to cum." He grabbed her hair and released all in her mouth. She swallowed every drop and kept sucking his dick and balls until it was hard again. Then she got on top of him and slid his dick inside of her.

Chapter Twenty-Six

Cordial counted out $50,000 in $100 dollar bills and placed them in a white envelope. He walked to his car, got in and pulled off. It was 9:30 that morning and he knew today could go either way for him. He saw the diner at the bottom of the street and a few men out front. He put his gun in the glove box and locked it then got out his car. Three guys pulled their guns out on him. He raised his hands to show he had no weapon and said, "I came to talk with Sammy. Pat him down on the inside."

When they patted him down one of the guys said, "he's clean. He only had this and held up the envelope with the money." They walked him to the back room where Sammy was at. When the door opened up, Sammy was smoking a cigar talking to Sunnie. When he saw Cordial, he looked at Sunnie and said, "Look, a dead man."

Cordial said, "I just came to talk that's all."

"Hey Sammy, he just had this on him."

Sammy reached for the envelope and looked inside and said, "A smart dead man. So, you came to talk? Have a seat.

Cordial looked around and sat down in front of Sammy at the desk. Sammy looked at his guys and said, "I'm good." They walked out. He then pulled his cigar and said, "Talk."

"I brought you $50,000 in cash. I got your message."

Sammy nodded his head at Sunnie, "What Fabio say?"

Cordial replied, "I got your message, Fabio didn't."

"So, who is this money coming from?" asked Sammy.

"It came from me."

"So why you pay me?" said Sammy.

"Because I know the rules to the game," said Cordial

"So, I'm taking it you are done with Fabio?"

"Yea, I have no more dealings with him, but I can't afford $50,000 a month. I can do $20,000 a month."

Sammy shook his head and said, "Why should I trust you?"

"Because I want to live my life without having to look over my shoulders," said Cordial.

"Does Fabio know you are here?" said Sunnie

"No, I haven't spoken to him in two days."

"Cordial, I'm going to let my better judgement get the best of me. From here on out you work for me, you understand?"

"Yes, I do," said Cordial.

Sammy took $15,000 dollars out and laid it on his desk and gave Cordial $35,000 back and said, "Every month I want $15,000." Cordial nodded his head.

Sammy said, "when I take Queens back, you will sell my product up there."

"Ok," said Cordial.

"One more thing," said Sammy. "Come see me a week from now."

Cordial nodded his head again and got up to leave.

Sammy said, "Don't make me regret this."

Cordial got back in his car and drove off. He knew what he did was fucked up but, fuck loyalty." Fabio said it best, 'know who you are dealing with and know when to fold.' And that's what he did.

Chapter Twenty-Seven

Fabio walked into his office and called Cordial a few times. When he didn't pick up, he knew then something was wrong. He walked to his office window and called Jamila.

"Hey, I was just about to call you. I'm walking in the restaurant now and I brought my friend Lorenzo with me."

"Ok, come upstairs," said Fabio.

"I'll be there in a few seconds."

After getting off the elevator Lorenzo said, "Damn, this place is fly."

"That's the same thing I said when I first came here," said Jamila.

Fabio was at the door waiting on them to walk in. "Hey bae, this is Lorenzo. Lorenzo this is Fabio."

"Nice to meet you."

"You too."

"Fabio this place is nice, "said Lorenzo.

"Thanks, I'm glad you like it."

"Jamila, Lorenzo, can I get you something to drink?"

"Yea, I'll take a shot of whatever," said Lorenzo.

"Jamila?"

"No, I'm good right now."

As Fabio was about to make the drink, his office phone started ringing.

"Lorenzo, give me one second on the drink. Hello."

"Mr. LaCross you have a Mr. Sammy Lenacci down here. He said he needs to talk with you."

Fabio looked at Jamila and Lorenzo and said, "Send them up."

"Yes sir."

Hanging up the phone he said, "I have someone coming up if you don't mind. I'll try and make it quick."

Jamila looked at him and said, "do you need us to leave?

"No, just have a seat." Fabio walked to the closet and pulled out a black .45 and placed it in the lower part of his back. Jamila watched him as he turned around, he saw her looking at him. That's when he heard a knock at the door. He walked to the door and opened it.

Sammy looked at him and said, "I guess this is how we have to meet now."

"I thought I made myself clear the last time we talked. Come have a seat," Fabio said. Lorenzo looked at everyone that walked in with Sammy. He knew something wasn't right. When Jamila saw Joey and Mark, she remembered them from the night they patted her down.

Fabio said, "this is Sammy, Sunnie, Mark, Joey and Bull. And this is Jamila and Lorenzo. So, Sammy, what can I do for you?"

"You mind if I smoke?" asked Sammy.

"No go ahead," said Fabio.

Sammy pulled his cigar out and started to lite it and said, "How many more people have to die Fabio? I'm giving you a chance to wipe the plate clean and start over."

Joey looked at Jamila and couldn't think where he knew her from.

Fabio said, "so you come up here with your goons hoping to intimidate me?"

Sammy said, "I remember over twenty years ago, Tony gave your father and mother the money to start this place up."

"Sammy, me, you and Tony had this conversation over and over again and my answer is still NO."

Jamila was watching everyone's movement as Fabio and Sammy talked.

"You think you are just a tough guy Fabio. Tony gave your poor ass father and mother the money to start this establishment up. Your father wasn't shit before Tony came into his life. He made your father and accepted you as his godson because you were all your father had to offer. You should be dead just like them."

"But I'm not and don't forget," Fabio said standing up with both hands on the table. "Tony looked in my father's eyes, shook his hand and had him killed. Him and my mother. So, when I went to his funeral, I went to see a dead man, not out of respect, but to see his lifeless body. And to know that he got his neck cut from ear to ear put a smile on my face knowing that fat son of a bitch died holding his fucking throat." Sammy's face was red.

Jamila and Joey caught eye contact. That's when he said, "It's her. She's the one, Sammy. That's the bitch that was with Tony that night". Sammy looked at her then Fabio and said, "you muthafucker." He jumped back from the table and pulled his gun out and shot at Fabio but missed. He hit Lorenzo in the shoulder. Lorenzo flipped back in the chair.

Sunnie pulled his gun out but Fabio shot at him making him duck. Joey ran and picked Jamila up and slammed her face down on the floor, kicking her in the stomach. Fabio looked at Joey beating on Jamila and pointed his gun at him. That's when Mark shot him two times in the chest and arm making him drop his gun. Lorenzo got up and hit Joey in the back with a chair. Joey fell to the ground. Sammy shot Lorenzo in the side, dropping him. Fabio's gun slid by Jamila and she picked it up from the floor and shot Mack in the head.

Sammy looked at her. She aimed the gun at him, and Bull jumped in front of him trying to move him out the way and got shot in the neck. Sammy shot at Jamila and just missed her. She jumped up and shot at him grazing him in the face. Sunnie grabbed him and pulled him out the door. Joey punched Jamila so hard in the face making her dizzy. She hit the floor. He picked her up off the floor with both hands wrapped around her throat. Not realizing she still had the gun in her hand, she put it to his face and pulled the trigger. Blood hit the wall and Joey's body dropped.

Jamila hit the floor hard trying to catch her breath. She looked over at Fabio bleeding laying on his side and Lorenzo laying on his back. Sammy and Sunnie were gone. Jamila dropped the gun and ran to Fabio and tried to pick him up. He sat up making a painful sound and said, "Check on Lorenzo." Lorenzo looked at Jamila and said, "I can't move my arm."

"Don't worry, I'll go get some help." said Jamila.

Fabio looked at her and said, "No, don't. Just lock the office door now.

Jamila ran and locked the office door.

"Now come and help me get Lorenzo up," said Jamila. "You and him are bleeding badly."

"We just need to make it to Frankie's house. We can go out the back way to my car," said Fabio.

Jamila took Lorenzo down first out the back and ran back up and got Fabio. Once in the car she said, "Where am I going?" "I-95 to exit 7 and make the first right." Fabio was in and out. Lorenzo passed out from the pain. Jamila pulled up to the white gates. When they opened, she drove down the driveway doing 90 mph. Frankie and his men ran out the house guns in their hands. He saw Fabio and Lorenzo and said, "What happened?"

Jamila said, "Sammy got them."

"Inside", Frankie yelled to the back now.

It was so much blood in the car. Jamila asked, "Are they going to make it?"

"We are going to try and save them. They lost a lot of blood," said Frankie

Jamila sat down with her hands on her head looking down at the ground. Frankie walked up to her sitting on the steps covered in blood.

"Jamila, how many men did Sammy have with him?" asked Frankie.

Jamila said without looking up at Frankie, "It was five of them and I killed three and shot Sammy in the face."

When Jamila said that Frankie turned around and walked off. He came back a few minutes later with a glass of water. "Jamila, have something to drink."

She reached for the glass from Frankie and said, "Thank you."

"You're welcome. So, tell me what happened?" Asked Frankie. "How did they get shot?"

Taking a sip of water, she said, "Fabio asked me to come by the restaurant. So, me and Lorenzo went and was talking to Fabio when he got a phone call saying Sammy is downstairs and needs to talk with him. The next thing I know they were talking about money to start a business and having his father killed. And Fabio being a godson to Tony. Words went back and forth. Sammy called Fabio a muthafucker and shot at him. From that point bullets went flying back and forth. Joey picked me up and slammed me on my face." Jamila looked up at Frankie and showed him the bruise on her face. "I just remember getting kicked over and over in the stomach. Then Fabio getting shot and falling down by me. I picked his gun up and from that point, I knew it was us or them. So, I killed one of them and tried to shoot Sammy. But someone jumped in front of him and I killed him. Sammy shot at me but missed. I hit him in the face. One of them grazed him. Sunnie, that's his name. I remember Fabio saying that he grabbed Sammy and ran out the door. Joey picked me up by the throat and I shot him point blank in the head killing him."

Frankie looked at her and said, "You're telling me there are three dead men laying there right now?"

"Yea, we left out the back door." Said Jamila.

Frankie told her to hold on one second. Frankie was talking to Marcus for a few seconds then Marcus left. Frankie walked back to Jamila and said, "Come inside and wash that blood off you and get something to eat."

Jamila got up and followed him inside.

SAYNOMORE

Chapter Twenty-Eight

Sammy didn't say a word walking in the diner holding a rag over his face. He walked in the back room, looked in the mirror and saw where Jamila shot him at. Sunnie walked in the backroom and said, "I called a meeting with everyone. I had Alex do it." Sammy turned around and looked at Sunnie with a long graze on his cheek. "That nigga shot me and if it wasn't for Bull, I would have been dead. She's got Tony's blood on her hands and Fabio had a part in it." Said Sammy.

"Sammy, Fabio is dead. You shot him. Mark shot him. I saw when his body hit the floor," Sunnie said.

Sammy flipped the desk over and kicked the chair over and said, "I want her fucking dead."

"She's good, really good. She got to Tony. She killed Bull, and Mark. And Joey didn't come out, so my guess is he's dead too. One shot, one kill. That's why I got you out of there Sammy," Sunnie told him.

Sammy looked at him and said, "Fabio was behind it all along. Make sure he is dead and find out who that Jamila bitch is and kill her."

Sunnie went to walk out the office and Sammy said to him, "Fuck a meeting, just get what I said done and get Cordial down here. He might know who that bitch is."

*****

Frankie walked to the back where Fabio and Lorenzo were at and asked April, "How are they doing?"

April looked at him and said, "they lost a lot of blood, but they are going to be fine." Looking at Fabio she said, "He's lucky the bullet just missed his liver by inches and the one to the breast plate. I got both bullets out. He's sleeping right now. This one is very lucky the bullet that went in his back, just missed his spin. The one to his arm went in and out, but like I said, they lost a lot of blood. I had to stop the bleeding on both of them first before I could do anything."

"How long before I can talk with them?" asked Frankie.

"I have both of them on morphine for the pain so give it a few hours."

"Thanks April," said Frankie

"No problem."

Frankie walked back in the den where Jamila was at. She was sleeping in his recliner. He looked at her and walked out to his desk and called Marcus.

"Yea," said Marcus

"Was it like she said?" asked Frankie.

"Just like it. Three of them. Joey lost the side of his face. Mark got the back of his head blown off and Bull got a neck shot. He choked on his own blood. I got all of them out there in the back of the truck and Ms. Simpson and her girls got the place cleaned up." said Marcus.

"How long before you get back?" asked Frankie

"It depends. Where do you want me to drop them off at?"

"Shit," said Frankie. "Put them in a dumpster across town somewhere and be done with it."

"I'll call you when I'm done," replied Marcus.

Frankie hung up the phone knowing the war Fabio just brought on himself. When he turned around Jamila was standing at the door looking at him. Frankie waved his hand for her to come outside with him.

"I came in there a few minutes ago but you were asleep." Said Frankie.

"I was for a minute. How is Fabio and Lorenzo?" asked Jamila.

"They are sleeping right now."

"So where do we go from here?" Asked Jamila

Frankie pulled his cigar and looked at Jamila and said, "Sammy's not going to stop until he kills you. Before today, have you killed anybody?"

"No," said Jamila, looking at Frankie in the eyes.

"How you learn to shoot like that?" asked Frankie

Mob Ties

"Me and Lorenzo use to go to the shooting range all the time every weekend," replied Jamila

"Well now, you are playing with fire and you killed Bull, Joey and Mark. You struck the first match," said Frankie. "Now it's kill or be killed."

Jamila had her arms crossed leaning against the rail. "You have to move smart. Sammy has a lot of people under his wing and you are a nobody. So, if someone thinks they can bring your head to him for a pot of gold, they are going to cash in on the check." Said Frankie.

"So how do I stop it?" asked Jamila

"You don't stop it, you kill it." said Frankie taking a pull of his cigar.

"What about Cordial and Tesfar? Those are his boys. When they find out, what happens when they pull up?" said Jamila.

"No, they are not. Tesfar got killed a few days ago and Cordial, I never trusted him. His handshake doesn't match his smile and I told Fabio that before. Cordial is yellow," said Frankie, putting the cigar out.

Jamila looked at her clothes and said, "Can you have someone take me to change clothes and to get my car?"

"Yea, but let me give you something first before you leave. Follow me."

Jamila followed Frankie in the house to the basement. He opened the door to a back room. There was a chest he opened and pulled out a black 9mm and a baby .38 and handed them to Jamila with two clips fully loaded. Frankie said, "you are going to need them. At this point trust no one Jamila, but the ones you bleed with."

SAYNOMORE

Chapter Twenty-Nine

Cordial walked in the back room at Sammy's diner. Sunnie was looking at him not saying a word. Sammy had his back facing Cordial. When he turned around, Cordial saw the graze on his face. Sammy walked around the desk and leaned against the front of his desk. Looking at Cordial he said, "Who is Jamila?"

"Some bitch Fabio met a few months ago," said Cordial.

"I'm asking you a very serious question and I need to know the truth."

Sammy looked dead in Cordial's eyes when he said, "Did you have your hands in Tony's death?"

Cordial looked at him and said, "the first time I heard about Tony's death was on the news the day after it happened."

"This nigga Jamila, Fabio met a few months ago had her hands in Tony's death. So, what I need from you is to kill her and make sure Fabio is dead," said Sammy.

Cordial looked at Sammy and said, "Fabio is dead."

"That's what you need to find out. I shot him and Mark shot him. We saw him go down, but we just need to know. You look like you feel some type of way?" said Sammy.

"No, fuck him and I'll kill that bitch after I find out if Fabio is dead or alive," said Cordial.

"Good you have seven days starting now. And when you kill her, bring me her body," said Sammy

Cordial nodded his head and walked out the room

*****

Frankie walked in the back room and saw Fabio laying down with his eyes open.

"How do you feel?" Frankie asked.

Fabio looked up to him and with a dry mouth said, "Like shit." Fabio tried to sit up but was in too much pain. He looked up at Frankie and said, "Where is Jamila?"

Frankie pulled a chair up and placed it next to Fabio's bed and said, "she's fine. She had some business to take care of. She will be back. She just left. "Fabio, do you trust her?"

"Yea, I do Frankie."

Frankie nodded his head and said, "do you remember what happened?"

"I just remember Jamila being kicked and me getting shot and waking up here."

"Fabio, Jamila saved you and Lorenzo's lives. It's because of her, you're still here. You started a war over pennies. This was the same shit that got your father killed and your mother with him."

Looking at Frankie, Fabio said, "I don't know what I'm going to do now. Jamila might get killed and her friend shot. Tesfar's dead and Cordial ain't picking up his phone. He might be dead."

"Fabio, I don't know if you realized this, but Jamila killed Bull, Joey and Mark over you. And she shot Sammy in the face. Carried you and Lorenzo out of there and got you here. What I don't agree with is you started a war over chump change. Sammy's going to try every little trick in the black book to see you killed. If he doesn't think you are dead already. What you need to do is disappear for a little while or you might end up dead."

Fabio looked at him and said, "So you are telling me to run?"

Frankie got up and said, "I feel like I'm talking to your father again. No, Fabio I'm not telling you to run. I'm telling you to be smart and get out of sight for a little while. You said you trust Jamila."

"Yea, I do." said Fabio.

"Listen to me, Fabio, give her the deed to Jelani's and let her run it. You go back to Paris. Sammy doesn't have the pull to get to you out there or manpower Tony had. That's your backyard Fabio. Don't worry about Jamila. I have a feeling she's going to be just fine. Fabio, I have never been so upset with you. But when you brought a black girl in my house, I was upset, but after talking with her, she doesn't have a ghetto mind. There's more to her than we know."

Fabio looked away from Frankie and said, "my father told me to always stand my ground."

"And now your father is six feet in the ground," Frankie said.

"Frankie, I love her."

"She's not going to be the first female you love or the last one," Frankie told him.

"So how do I disappear?" asked Fabio.

"Fake your death and I will help you."

Looking at Frankie he said, "Why can't you help me with this war?"

"Fabio, it's not that I can't, but I made a truce with the Lenacci family two years ago and I have to honor my end. Don't get me wrong, we are not allying. We just have a truce that's all I can help you with. I will help you as much as I can to stay alive, but I can't get involved in a war."

Fabio picked himself up and said, "What about the bodies at the restaurant?"

"I took care of that already," said Frankie.

Fabio knew Frankie was right and if he stayed, it might cost Jamila her life. He said to Frankie, "I'll fake my death."

SAYNOMORE

Chapter Thirty

After getting out the shower Jamila looked at her wet body in the mirror. Staring at the bruise on her face was a reminder of yesterday. She put on a gray sweatshirt and her gray and white Jordan's. Looking at the guns Frankie gave her she put the 9mm on her waist and the baby .38 in her bag. Walking out her house to her car she knew what Frankie said was right, trust no one.

Pulling up at Nayana's house, she got out of her car and knocked on her door. Nayana opened the door and gave Jamila a hug and asked, "Where have you been?"

"Around," said Jamila.

"Oh my God, what happened to your face Jamila?"

"Long story but, I'm ok."

"Where is Cordial at?" asked Jamila

"I don't know. I haven't seen him all day," said Nayana.

"Well, you want to go get something to eat?" asked Jamila.

"Hold that thought, I have to use the bathroom," said Nayana.

She ran in the bathroom and closed the door. That's when her phone went off. Jamila looked and it was a message from Cordial.

"I'm going to be late coming in tonight. Sammy got me checking some things out for him and you were right about pulling back from Fabio. I'll let you know what's going on when I get in tonight."

Jamila read the text and looked back at the bathroom door. She knew now Cordial was working with Sammy and Nayana knew more than she put on. Jamila walked to the living room and sat down on the love seat. Nayana came out of the bathroom and said, "So what you want to get something to eat?"

Jamila looked at her and said, "Maybe some other time. I have to make a run I forgot about and your phone was going off too when you were in the bathroom. What you are doing later I'll stop by tonight."

"Call first," said Nayana. "I might be busy."

"Let me guess, that was your boo thing," said Jamila.

"No, it's Kim's boring ass telling me to call her."

Jamila got up and gave Nayana a kiss on the forehead and said, "I will." She looked at Nayana from her car before driving. Jamila hoped she didn't have to kill a friend knowing now Cordial is playing both sides and Nayana was with him.

*****

Frankie saw when Jamila's car pulled up. He was outside waiting on her when she walked up to him and said, "Is everything alright?"

"Jamila, Lorenzo pulled through he's inside eating now. But Fabio didn't make it. He died a few hours ago. His body couldn't take the loss of blood. He went into shock and there wasn't anything we could do to save him."

Jamila had tears in her eyes and said, "Can I see him?"

"Sure, come on."

Frankie took her in the back room and pulled the sheet from over his head. Jamila touched his hand and kissed his lips and said, "I promise you I swear to you I will kill Sammy and every one of them, Cordial and all. You will not die alone." She kissed his forehead and said, "I love you Fabio." She looked at Frankie and walked out.

"Jamila", Frankie called her.

She stopped and looked at him, "yes?"

"I was with him when his body went into shock. He told me before to give you the restaurant and that he loves you. I will have all the paperwork done within the next couple of weeks for you," said Frankie.

"Thank you but that restaurant won't bring him back to me." Then she walked off to see Lorenzo. Lorenzo was sitting in a chair looking out the window at the lake when Jamila walked in.

"Lorenzo, are you ok?"

"I am. How you feel? I'm sorry about Fabio."

"Thank you, Lorenzo. You ready to go home?" Asked Jamila.

"Yea, I am." Jamila helped him up and walked to the front of the house where Frankie was at. Lorenzo shook his hand and said, "Thank you."

"No problem," said Frankie.

After getting Lorenzo in the car, Jamila walked back in the house and asked Frankie for Fabio's phone. He looked at her and said, "What do you plan to do with it?"

"Cordial is working with Sammy," said Jamila.

"And how do you know this Jamila?"

"He sent a text to Nayana's phone and I saw it. So, I need Fabio's phone to set him up to meet me somewhere tonight." Said Jamila.

Frankie asked, "When you meet him then what?"

"I'll kill him first and send his head to Sammy."

Frankie walked out the room and got Fabio's phone and handed it to her. "Whatever you need, call me. If I can help I will."

"Thank you," said Jamila before walking out to her car.

Lorenzo looked at Jamila and said, "I saw that look in your eyes before. "

"They killed a man I loved. They shot Elisha and killed his family and tried to kill me and you. It's time we hit back now. Are you with me?" asked Jamila.

"I'm always with you, hands down. So, what do you want to do first?" asked Lorenzo.

"I'll drop you off at home and let you know later tonight."

SAYNOMORE

Chapter Thirty-One

Cordial walked into Nayana's house and gave her a hug.
"So, what is it you had to tell me?" she asked Cordial.
"I'm not going to sugar coat it. Sammy is giving me Queens, but he wants Fabio and Jamila dead. He wants me to bring her body to him after I kill her. She had her hands in Tony's death and he wants her dead for it. Now I'll have to pay him $15,000 a month but I'll be bringing in $30,000 a month. I know that's your girl so I'm just being real with you," said Cordial.
Nayana grabbed his hand and said, "that's my girl but you are my man. She chose Fabio and I chose you. So just tell me what I need to do, and it's done."
"I need her to meet me somewhere either tonight or tomorrow night," said Cordial. "And I'll do the rest. I only have seven days Sammy told me."
"I'll tell her to pick me up wherever you tell me to, and you just do the rest," said Nayana.
"That's why you are my down ass bitch."
At that time Cordial got a text to his phone. "We need to talk. Can you pull behind the warehouse by the docks around 12 midnight?
"Shit, Fabio's texting me now." said Cordial
"Yea, I got you bro, I'll be there. Damn, I'm glad you're good," Cordial text back.
"Baby be safe," Nayana said as he walked out the house. It was already 10:30pm. He wanted to make sure he was on point.

*****

It was a cold breeze coming off the Hudson as Cordial threw rocks in the river waiting on Fabio. When he turned around, he saw Jamila's car pull up. She got out and walked to him. She had the same gray sweatsuit on.
"Where's Fabio?" Cordial asked.

Jamila looked at him and said, "he took too many shots in the chest and liver. His body gave up on him."

"So, you were the one texting me?" Said Cordial.

"Yea, I need you to deliver a message for me."

Cordial looked at her and said, "Bitch, who the fuck you think I am? Deliver a message?" Before he saw it Jamila pulled out her 9mm and pointed it at his head and said, "I'm the bitch who just killed you."

"What the fuck you are doing Jamila?" said Cordial.

"It's Jamila. Not bitch, hun."

"Fuck you and Sammy. I'll send him your best wishes." Cordial went to jump at her and she shot him three times in the chest. He fell on his knees and she shot him one more time in the back of the head. His body hit the ground. She shot him again. That's when she heard noises from behind and she pointed her gun at two men walking up to her.

"It's Marcus, don't shoot."

"Why the fuck you are following me?" said Jamila

"I'm not. This is Frankie's warehouse. We saw the whole thing. I came down to help you get rid of the body," Marcus told her.

"How did you know it was me?" asked Jamila

"Your car is the only reason we didn't shoot at you. And then when you got out, I saw it was you."

"So why you ain't shoot Cordial?" she asked Marcus

"I wanted to see who he was meeting first."

Jamila looked around and said, "I need his head and phone before you dump the body." Marcus handed her phone. Jamila was looking in Cordial's messages for a message from Sammy. When she says Nayana's text, "let me know when you want me to call Jamila and have her meet up with you somewhere. I'm waiting on you, bae." The text was an hour ago. Jamila looked at the text again knowing her best friend was down to get her killed over some dick. Jamila replied, "have her meet you at the house in one hour and I'll be there." Ok, was the reply.

Jamila walked to Marcus, "I have to take care of something. You got this?"

"Yea, you are coming back?" asked Marcus
"In like an hour and a half," said Jamila
That's when her phone went off.
"Hello. What's up?"
"What you doing, Jamila?" asked Nayana
"Nothing beautiful." said Jamila
"Are you still coming over?"
"Yea, I'm on my way now," replied Jamila
Jamila pulled out her baby .38 and placed it in her pocket. She was outside Nayana's front door. After quickly checking her surrounding, she opened the door.
"What's up beautiful?" said Jamila. Nayana was on the phone texting when she walked in.
You want something to drink?" asked Nayana
"No thanks."
Jamila looked at Cordial phone and saw the text Nayana sent her, "How long before you get here?" Nayana sat down at the table and said, "you never told me what happened to your face."
Jamila looked at her and said, "Cordial's not coming, he's dead."
Nayana looked at her and said, "What are you talking about?"
"I know you tried to set me up from the very beginning. When I was here earlier when you got a text and said it was Kim. I knew then it was from Cordial and how you just texted him. See here, how long before you get here."
Jamila showed Nayana his phone and stood up. Nayana looked at the phone and yelled. "Get the fuck out my spot." she picked up the kitchen knife.
Jamila pulled out her gun and said, "I am".
Nayana said, "Please don't. Please don't Jamila." Jamila let a tear fall from her eye and shot Nayana two times in the chest and walked over to her. As her body was on the floor, she shot Nayana in the face and said, "You two-faced bitch." Then she turned around and left out the house.

SAYNOMORE

Chapter Thirty-Two

"Alex, I want that bitch dead, you hear me?" Sammy slammed his fist down on the desk. "That nigga bitch shot me in the fucking face. I want her dead."

"I have a team looking for her now," said Sunnie.

"Call that cop ummm. What's his name?" said Sammy.

"Omar," Sunnie said

Sammy said, "Get him down here. He needs to put some work in for the family." There was a knock at the door. "Who the fuck is it?" yelled Sammy.

"John. Boss, you have a package at the door."

"Well bring it to me. It's no damn good at the door now is it?" When Sammy opened the box, it was Cordial's head. He jumped back and said, 'Fuck." Sunnie looked and said, "There's a note inside." He pulled the note out and read it:

"Sammy, get my message. You fucked up. (LF)."

"What the fuck do LF mean? Find out who killed him and sent me this message, said Sammy.

Sammy took a napkin and wiped his face and said, "get rid of this." Alex picked the box up and walked out. "Sunnie do we know if Fabio is dead?" asked Sammy.

"He's dead, Sammy. From what I was told his body is on an ice tray. His whole family is dead."

"So, who has the restaurant now?" asked Sammy.

"I don't know. Find out for me. The Lenacci Family can't afford to look weak. I want everything burned down. His house, restaurant everything. And that family who we killed, the boy in the coma, find out who visits him and bring them to me. We need to get our point across on what happens when you fuck with the Lenacci family."

*****

Jamila called Lorenzo. "Hello," he answered.

"Hey, look this is what I need you to do. Can you find out where Alex or Sunnie live or be at?" asked Jamila.

"I have a few people who might know something," said Lorenzo.

"Find out. I need to know this yesterday. Call me back when you do," said Jamila before hanging up the phone. Jamila pulled up at Frankie's house and when he saw her, he said, "I was just asking myself when you were going to come see me."

"I should have come by to see you sooner," said Jamila. "There was so much going on from Elisha's being shot to Fabio being killed. To me killing five people in the last couple of weeks."

"Jamila in this life people die all the time. My question is after all this is done, what are you going to do?" said Frankie. "You can't go back to your old life. You have too much blood on your hands. The first time I saw you the look on your face as you looked at the picture of Tony Lenacci. Your face gave out a sign now I'm asking you, how do you know Tony?" asked Frankie.

Jamila looked at Frankie and took a deep breath and said, "I was the one who tied him up."

Frankie looked at her and said, "You are telling me you did what the Scott family couldn't do and the Deniro family. Tony was the untouchable Don to most. That is a very strong accusation Jamila.

"Do you think I would lie to you, Frankie?" said Jamila

"No but look at it from my point of view. There are a lot of people trying to find out what happened. Who killed the Boss of Bosses Jamila," said Frankie?

"Frankie, I don't like to talk about the things that I do but for you I will show you this one time. Then from here on out you could take my word if you chose too. And I hope after this you will never question me again."

"Show me what?" Frankie said.

Jamila pulled out her phone and showed him the picture of Tony still alive tied up to a chair with his dick hanging out. Frankie couldn't believe what he was seeing.

"How were you able to get close to him?" asked Frankie.

"I have a pussy Frankie," said Jamila

Frankie knew then that Jamila was a true killer. "Has anybody else seen these pictures?", asked Frankie.

"No just you."

"Jamila hold on," Frankie got up and walked in the back room and came back out a few minutes later. "Before Fabio died, he wanted me to give you this."

"What is this?" Jamila asked.

"Open it and look."

Jamila opened it and he saw the deed to Jelani's and a check for $3,000,000 dollars.

"Make him proud and finish what you started. Make a name for yourself. From day one, I saw something in you, and I was right. I hope I see good things from you and now Jamila, you have an ally with me and my family. Kill the head and the body will fall Jamila," said Frankie.

"Thank you, Frankie and I will." Jamila got up and walked outside to her car and said the LaCross Family to herself.

SAYNOMORE

Chapter Thirty-Three

Isaiah was leaving the hospital with his girlfriend Kim. "So how much longer do you think he's going to be in a coma?" Kim asked. "I don't know, he's in a lot of pain," said the doctor. "And lost a lot of blood."

"Come on. Let's go get something to eat," said Isaiah when they went to get in the car, a black van pulled up when the sliding doors opened, three men jumped out with mask on holding AR-15's in their hands. They smacked Isaiah in the face with the gun and grabbed Kim by her hair and threw them both in the van. As they pulled off Kim dropped her bag by the car.

"Please don't hurt me," she cried. "Please don't."

"Shut the fuck up", one of the guys said to her.

Isaiah had a gun in his face. He didn't say a word. One of the guys said, "Make the call and let them know we will be going to field forty-eight. We will be there in twenty minutes."

Isaiah knew this was the same people who shot Elisha and killed his family. Looking at Kim scared for her life made him mad knowing she was going to die. He felt bumps in the road for five minutes then the van stopped, and the doors opened.

"Get out," one of the guys said. All you saw corn fields for miles. Sammy was looking at them when they got out the van. He walked up to Isaiah and said, "I guess you are friends with Elisha's. So, tell me, were you in the club the night Tony was killed?" asked Sammy.

"I don't know what you are talking about. I was just visiting a friend of mine," Isaiah said.

"That's all."

Sammy looked at Alex and he smacked Isaiah in the face with the bat he had in his hand. When Isaiah hit the ground, Alex hit him in the back over and over again. Isaiah was screaming from the pain. "That's enough," said Sammy.

Isaiah was on his side trying to catch his breath.

"Let's try this again. Were you in the club the night Tony got killed?" he yelled.

Isaiah was laughing on the ground with blood coming from his face when he said, "I was there when Tony's fat ass was killed, when Jamila tied him up."

Sammy started kicking Isaiah in the face with the back of his heel. Alex put a rope around his neck choking him while Sammy beat him. Isaiah's body was black and blue with mud and blood all over him. Kim was screaming and crying watching the whole thing. They beat and raped Kim for over an hour before beating her like they did Isaiah. They stripped them down to nothing and took Isaiah's phone and found Jamila's number. They sent pictures of them beaten to death with broken bones laying in mud and blood to Jamila's phone. Both bodies were black and blue all over. Then they dumped their bodies in a hole and drove off making sure Jamila got the message.

*****

Jamila called Lorenzo and told him to come to Jelani's. When he got there, she was sitting at the table drinking a shot of Grey Goose.

"Last time I was here I almost died." Said Lorenzo.

"We were lucky. I wish I could say the same thing about Isaiah and Kim," replied Jamila.

"What do you mean, Jamila?" asked Lorenzo.

Jamila slid her phone over to Lorenzo and showed him the pictures.

"Who sent you these?"

"Sammy from Isaiah's phone. I got them last week," replied Jamila. "They beat them in a fucking field." Jamila threw her glass across the room to the wall. "I want him fucking dead, Lorenzo. Dead."

"Jamila, cool down."

"How Lorenzo?"

Jamila closed her eyes and said, "Did you find out where Sunnie or Alex be?"

"Yea," said Lorenzo. "There's a bar in downtown Manhattan that Sunnie goes to. He gambles at the poker tables."

Jamila walked across the room and said, "Kidnap him. I want him alive."

Lorenzo poured himself a shot of gin and said, "Where do you want me to bring him after I kidnap him?"

"Remember that farm we use to shoot at when we were younger? Bring him there, and we need more men. We can't win a war just the two of us. We need loyal men, Lorenzo."

"I know a few guys who use to work security who are used to violence. They are down for whatever as long as they are getting paid," said Lorenzo.

Jamila said, "your father was a mobster. I remember going to that night club with you being the only black person there. But you never treated me different and you never got involved in that life. Why?"

"Because the things I saw and witnessed, it's a cutthroat underground world. My father is doing life in prison now behind the Mob, Jamila."

"And Lorenzo," said Jamila. "You know I'm starting my own Mob family and you are standing here with me why?"

"Because I've been standing with you from day one, twenty-two years ago and you never changed on me," said Lorenzo.

Jamila looked at him and said, "I killed Nayana. What you have to say about that?"

Lorenzo looked at her and said, "Who am I to question what you do? What's done is done. I'll go get those men and bring them back here."

"Yea," said Jamila. "Bring them back here but call me first. I'll go check on Elisha, and Lorenzo..."

"Yea," said Lorenzo.

"We are the LaCross family now."

*****

Jamila walked in the hospital and up to the visitor's desks. "Hello, I'm here to see Elisha McGhee. My name is Jamila Cotwel." The nurse looked on the computer and said, "I'm sorry. He is no longer here."

"What do you mean he's no longer here?" asked Jamila.

"Hold on. Let me get someone who can help you, ma'am. If you don't mind having a seat over there."

A few minutes later a Dr. Bowden approached her. "Hi, I'm Dr. Bowden and you are?"

"Jamila Cotwel."

"How do you know Elisha, Ms. Cotwel?"

"We grew up together," said Jamila.

We'll Ms Cotwel, Elisha woke up out of the coma a week ago and yesterday he pulled his IV's out. That's all we know. We do have him leaving on video tape but that's all."

"Oh my God," cried Jamila

"Ms. Cotwel, if you find him, he needs to get back here for more testing as soon as possible."

"Ok, thank you," said Jamila as she walked out the doors. "Where could he have gone? Where could he be?" Jamila rode around for two hours looking for him.

Chapter Thirty-Four

Sunnie looked at Alex and said, "Did you ever find Elisha?"
"Ever since he left the hospital, I don't know where he's at. We have been looking everywhere."
Sunnie walked up to Alex and put his hands on his shoulders and said, "Did you go back to his house?"
"No, I didn't think he would go back there," replied Alex.
"Hey you never know." Sunnie moved his hands off of Alex's shoulder and walked off.
"I will take a few men and go by there tomorrow," said Alex.
Sunnie replied, "Why do it tomorrow when you can do it today?"
Alex got up and said, "I'm on it now."

*****

Jamila picked up the phone and called Lorenzo.
"Hey, How's Elisha?" asked Lorenzo.
"He's gone Lorenzo."
"What you mean he's gone?" said Lorenzo.
"He took his IV's out and left the hospital. I've been looking for him for two hours now," said Jamila.
"Jamila you think he might have gone home?"
"I don't know. I ain't think about that. Let me go by there and check and I'll let you know Lorenzo."
Why didn't I think of that?
As Jamila pulled up to Elisha's house, she could still see the blood stained on the pavement. Before she went in the house, she got down on one knee and said the Lord's Prayer for Elisha's family and Abby. When she got up, she saw the blinds moving and asked herself, "Could Elisha be inside?" When she pushed open the door, she called out his name.
"Elisha are you in here? It's me Jamila. Elisha." She made her way upstairs and peeked in a room and said, "It's me Jamila, Elisha." She heard a noise coming from down the hallway and

followed it to his little brother's room. She found Elisha laying on the floor holding a picture of his family crying and rocking back and forth apologizing. Jamila dropped her purse and ran over to him and you. Elisha was still crying holding his family picture saying no. All Jamila could do was hold him and say, "I'm here for you now."

She sat there for about thirty-five minutes holding him while he cried.

"Elisha, did you hear that?" said Jamila as she looked out the window and saw Alex and three of his guys walking to the house. She ran back to Elisha, "Get up, we have to go now."

*****

"Someone is here, Alex," One of the men whispered.

"I can see that, Roc. You two go around back and you come with me," Alex instructed.

*****

"Elisha come on. Come on." Jamila helped Elisha up then pulled her gun out her purse. "Shhh."

Alex walked in the house and looked up the stairs. "If you don't want to die, state your name. We just want one person."

Elisha was still in much pain as Jamila tried to hold him up against the wall.

Alex pointed upstairs and one of the guys started slowly walking up them. Jamila pulled Elisha back without saying a word. She turned the corner in the hallway and shot the intruder twice, sending him back down the stairs to Alex. Alex started shooting at her and she was shooting back at him. The other two men ran to the front where Alex was at.

Alex yells, "They're upstairs."

"Damn," Jamila said. "It's three of them, Elisha."

Jamila looked around for a way out. Alex yelled to her. "I hope you know you are a dead bitch."

Jamila threw a clock out the window breaking the glass. Alex ran outside with one of the guys as one of them went upstairs. Jamila heard him coming and shot at him but missed. He shot Jamila in the leg making her fall backwards. As he ran upstairs, Jamila shot him in the face dropping him.

"Elisha come on, we have to go now," says Jamila. Elisha was still weak from being shot and being in a coma as she got him downstairs, they made it to the front door. Alex shot at them but missed. He told one guy to go around back so they couldn't get out. Jamila saw the man run and started shooting at Alex so Elisha could make it to the car.

Jamila yelled, "Get in," as she continued shooting at Alex. Jamila ran for the car and Alex's man shot at her knocking the back window out of her car. Jamila got in the car and took off hitting Alex's car trying to get away. Alex shot the side window out as she took off.

Elisha, "Are you ok?" asked Jamila

"Yea, who was that Jamila?"

"The people who killed your family and now they want me and you are dead too.

"Jamila are you ok?" asked Elisha.

"Yea, they shot me in my leg. We need to pull over somewhere."

Alex got in his car to chase them, but they were nowhere to be. Jamila lost them as they made it back to the restaurant. As she pulled up, Lorenzo ran outside. "What happened?" Lorenzo asked as he ran to Jamila.

"You've been shot." said Lorenzo.

"Don't worry about me, help Elisha inside." Replied Jamila.

"Come on Elisha," Lorenzo said as he helped him out the car. He looked back at Jamila and said, "Are you alright?"

"Yea," said Jamila. "It went in and out. I'm fine. I went to Elisha's house. They must have been watching it because I wasn't there for an hour. They came to kill me."

"Let's get this leg taken care of and we will deal with that later," said Lorenzo.

SAYNOMORE

Chapter Thirty-Five

Alex called Sammy. Sammy picked up after the second ring.
"Yea," he said.
"They were there boss."
"Did you take care of them?" asked Sammy
"No, we got flatlined."
"Come to the bar now," said Sammy.
John asked, "What did Sammy say?"
"Come to the bar now," Alex told him.
"What happened now?" Sunnie asked.
"She killed two more of our men then got away."
"This bitch is starting to get under my fucking skin," said
Sunnie. "The bitch just won't fucking die."
"Relax Sammy. Let's just hear what Alex has to say when he
gets back," said Sunnie taking a shot of gin.
Alex walked through the doors thirty minutes later. Sammy
looked at him and said, "Is it that hard to kill a bitch?"
"Sammy, we got there, and it was just a big shootout. There
wasn't shit we could do in an open neighborhood. It wasn't a win,
win situation for us at all." Sammy looked at John and Alex and
said, "Get the fuck out before I fucking kill both of you now."

*****

"Jamila, remember the guys I was talking to you about
yesterday?" said Lorenzo.
"Yea, I remember."
"They are here." Said Lorenzo
"Bring them up and let me meet them," said Jamila.
Jamila was walking with a limp from being shot. She sat behind
the oakwood desk waiting to see who Lorenzo had for her. That's
when she saw three guys walk in. One guy was a heavyset, bald-
headed white guy about six foot one. The other one looked to be
five foot nine with short hair, goatee and weighed about two
hundred pounds, he was black. The last one was a pretty boy. He

was six feet with longhair Italian. Lorenzo says, "Chad, Shawn, and Nick, meet Jamila."

"Nice to meet you. I'm glad you were able to stop by."

"Nice to meet you too Jamila. May I have a seat?"

"Please do all of you."

"So, Ms. LaCross," said Lorenzo. "You were looking for some loyal guys."

"I am," said Jamila.

"Good because we are looking for a loyal family."

"Chad, my family is small, but we stand on loyalty, trust, honor and respect. And I take very good care of my men."

Nick looked at her and said, "What are the rules?"

"I'm the only chief and Lorenzo is my number two man. Family over everything. We don't back down and we don't take disrespect from nobody."

"Do you have room for more men?" Nick asked.

"Yea, I do. Have them talk to Lorenzo. So, I'm taking it you all want to be a part of this family?" asked Jamila.

"Yea we are," said Chad.

Jamila stood up and shook their hands and said, "you come see me tomorrow at 2 pm. And one more thing after today, this is where I need you at."

*****

It had been two weeks since Jamila's been shot. She stopped by Frankie's to see him.

"Mr. Landon you have a visitor."

"Show them to the pool and I'll be back there in a few minutes."

Ms. Simpson looked and said, "Jamila, follow me this way."

As Jamila sat down by the pool Frankie walked up and said, "Nice to see you again Jamila."

"It's nice to see you too Frankie," as she got up and gave him a hug and a kiss on the cheeks.

"So, I was watching the news Jamila and I saw two dead bodies being carried out of your friend's house a few days ago. Do you have anything to say about that?" asked Frankie.

Jamila grinned and said, "Self-defense."

"I had a feeling you had something to do with that. I'm glad you stopped bye. Because I needed to talk with you." Frankie lit his cigar and said, "so word is that Sammy had a head sent to him with the letters, "LF" on a note."

Jamila looked at him and said, "I think I heard something like that too."

As Frankie blew smoke out his mouth he said, "What do "LF" mean?"

"The LaCross Family, Frankie."

"So, you are taking on Fabio's family name?" asked Frankie

"It's only right. The Lenacci family killed his mother, father and him. It's only right to carry on his name."

Frankie pulled his cigar and nodded his head and said, "Jamila," Fabio supplied 75% of Queens. That's why he was able to hold on to the city. If you are not supplying the city, someone else is going to try and take over your turf." Said Frankie.

"Frankie, I don't know where Fabio kept his cocaine or who he dealt with," said Jamila.

"Jamila, Fabio kept a login book of everything and if I know him it's somewhere in his office. It's up to you to find it. Being the head of a family, you have to make sure everyone eats at your table," said Frankie.

"I understand, but I'm at war right now with a very powerful family."

"Trust me Jamila, that war is not going to stop no time soon. Find the book and take care of the city." Jamila got up and said, "I'll be back next week." Jamila said. "Frankie everyone is talking about how you came out of nowhere and you ain't taking no shit from the Lenacci family. And how you had Tony killed. They respect you." Jamila smiled and walked off.

Once back at Jelani's, Jamila sat down at her office desk and looked around and said, "Where is that book at?" She got up and looked everywhere for hours. She was looking at his birdcage and got up and walked inside it. She walked to the back wall and noticed a door. She pushed it open and it was a hidden office with cameras showing every area in the restaurant. On his desk was his login book and another book with people who owed him. It was also a key to a warehouse in Long Island. She took the books and key and left out the office and sat down at her desk. Jamila went over everything Fabio had and noticed he had over $500,000 in cash owed to him. He also supplied judges, cops, people from the mayor's administration and even a few local dealers. He had written down what they would get on a monthly basis. Fabio's been dead over four months now. Jamila called Lorenzo and told him she needed to see him ASAP and that she had a few jobs for him to take care of. After getting off the phone with him, she called every number in the book to let the ones who owed her, know that she would be collecting this week. She let the others know she was taking over where Fabio left off at. All the numbers were still the same and within the hour, she had over twenty orders and people to meet to find out who she was. She got up, picked up her car keys and drove off to Long Island to see what was in the warehouse.

*****

Looking around Jamila saw a building that looked old but in good shape. There were a few warehouses around, but each warehouse was a good distance away from each other. She walked to the front door and used the key she got from Fabio's office to open the door. The warehouse was empty beside some pallets that were stacked up on the side of the wall. Six barrels lined up in one of the corners. There were also other barrels that were used to catch water from the leaking roof. She walked in every room, but she knew just like Fabio had a hidden office, he has a hidden room somewhere in here too. "Where is it at?" Jamila said to herself. She doubled back to every room she went in. The only noise you heard were her heels as she walked the floor in the empty building. She walked over to the barrels lined up on the wall and opened one to see what was inside. When she opened it a thick cloud of smoke came out. As she looked, it was filled with cocaine that hadn't been cut yet. She opened up all the barrels to make sure. She closed them back and locked the door to the warehouse. She called Lorenzo and told him she wanted to see him and everyone else at Jelani's tomorrow at 1p.m.

SAYNOMORE

Chapter Thirty-Six

Lorenzo called Jamila and told her to meet him at the Olive Garden. When she walked in, he was already at a table waiting on her.

"What's up Lorenzo?" said Jamila

"Nothing. I got us this private booth. So, what's up?"

"I wanted to know what you wanted to talk about tomorrow." Asked Lorenzo

"I found Fabio's cocaine and I talked to Frankie earlier today," said Jamila. "He made a good point to me." Lorenzo sat back and just listened. "If I'm going to keep a hold onto Queens like Fabio did, I have to supply Queens. I found the book of everybody who owes him and everybody he did business with. I need you to go make the collection for me. I'll meet some of the people he did business with tomorrow."

"So, we really don't have to have this meeting tomorrow. If you give me the names and places, I can take care of that first thing tomorrow."

Jamila handed the book and said, "Have Chad and Nick meet me at Jelani's in the morning around ten."

"They will be there," Lorenzo said. "Now let's order."

*****

Omar walked in the office and sat down.

"Thanks for coming to see me," Sammy said, smoking his cigar.

So, "What seems to be the problem?" asked Omar

I have a female trying to take over Fabio's turf. I need her to disappear. Wrap her body in plastic and throw it in the Hudson. There's a picture of her. Here, Sammy slides a picture of Jamila and an envelope with $20,000 in it on the table. Omar looked at the money and put the envelope in his pocket and said, she will be dead by the end of the week.

Sammy looked at him as he walked out and said, Sunnie now my itch is gone.

Don't count your eggs before they hatch. She's smarter than we think. She knows how to move, said Sunnie.

So did Fabio but now he's dead Sammy said.

*****

Jamila looked at Dapp and said, "You come see me. The numbers will never change."

"How do I know it's the same product? You can say the numbers will never change, but it can be a lower grade coke. I spend up to $150,000 for the A-1 so again, how do I know it's the same?" asked Dapp.

Jamila looked at Chad and said, "Hand me that bag over there." When Chad got back with the bag, Jamila took out a Ziplock bag and slid it across the table to Dapp. He opened the bag and sniffed a line and said, "Now this is what the fuck I'm talking about. Let me get six of them."

"They will be ready tomorrow no later than 2 p.m. and that's $150,000," said Jamila.

Dapp got up and said, "I'll be back tomorrow." Jamila shook his hand and said, "I'll see you then."

Watching Dapp leave, she knew she opened up a new door. She had a team chopping and weighing up the cocaine even bagging it up, her seal was a broken diamond. She had Nick over seeing them with Elisha running it. Lorenzo was collecting for her with Shawn. It's been a few days and no word from Sammy. Chad had a few more loyal men come talk to her. Jamila had two men downstairs walking around with Elisha and one as her driver. She knew it was a kill or be killed game. Now one rule she set was she would never break. First time you fuck up you die. She knew the restaurant would cover up her drug money and she would have to be behind the scenes to not have her face known. She needed fourteen kilos. She walked out to her car with Chad and he opened her car door for her to get in.

*****

Omar was down the street watching as they drove off. He followed them down a few blocks before her driver saw him.

"We have a car following us, Ms LaCross. He's been following us for fifteen minutes now."

"Pull over somewhere out of sight where no one can see us, but make sure he is still behind us," said Jamila. She reached in her purse and pulled out her black 9mm and put one in the chamber. There was an old gas station that was run down; it had flat pieces of wood covering the windows. Jamila's car pulled up at the gas station and the brown Toyota pulled over behind them. "Tim don't cut the car off, keep it running. Don't get out of the car. Watch everything from the rearview. If you can, get a picture of whoever gets out the car."

Jamila opened the car door and stepped out the car gun tucked behind her bag and waist. She closed the car door and looked at the brown Toyota. She walked to the car door and leaned against it. Omar opened his door and stepped out gun in his hand. He looked at Jamila and walked up to her and said, "so your driver is not getting out?"

"I told him not to because I don't see a threat." said Jamila. "So, I'm taking it you come to kill me and showing me your badge to let me know you're a cop."

"This can go two ways Jamila. One, you can pay me double the amount Sammy paid me or two, you can try and figure out which way I might come at you," said Omar.

"How much?" said Jamila

"$40,000," Omar said, never taking his eyes off Jamila.

"How long do I have to pay you? Forty-eight hours? Is there a number I can reach you at?" asked Jamila, as he started walking back to his car.

"No. And make it all $100's. It's easier to count that way. I'll be in touch," he said over his shoulder.

Jamila watched as he drove off knowing if she killed a cop, what type of heat that would bring on her. But she also knows that he can have her killed at a drop of a dime. Plant a gun on her and just like that, it's a justified killing and her ass on an ice tray. She got back in the car and told Tim to let her see the pictures he took of the officer.

"Do you want me to head to the warehouse Ms. LaCross?" Tim asked.

"No, head back to Jelani's. We have a big problem that needs to be taken care of ASAP." said Jamila.

Jamila pulled out her phone and called Lorenzo and told him she needs fourteen kilos tomorrow before 1 p.m. She walked in the restaurant and had Tim and Chad follow her to the office. She looked at them and said, "have a seat. What I'm about to ask you two has to be done right. *No slip-ups.* I need this officer to disappear with no blood spilled, no DNA. I need it done clean. His house burned down. We will not fold, and the Lenacci Family will not push us around. When this is over, blood will be in the mud, but it won't be our blood. I'm not the bad guy but muthafuckers only respect violence." Jamila stood up and said, "Tony is dead, so you know what that means. They bleed just like us."

Chad looked at Jamila and said, "Sammy is the head and Sunnie is his second in command. And Alex is his third. Sammy's not going to make any moves without Sunnie's knowledge and Sunnie likes to gamble downtown Manhattan. He's a big poker player. He never misses a game."

"How many men does he have with him? And where in downtown Manhattan?" Asked Jamila.

"It's a sports bar right off Lincoln Ave and my guess would be three maybe four of them at the most."

Jamila walked over to the window and said, "Let's get Sunnie first and then we deal with the cop."

Tim looked at Jamila and said, "why not kill two birds with one stone?"

She looked at him and said, "Sunnie's body could fall right on the DA's desk and it will be just another murder case. But the N.Y.C. Officer would be breaking news, C.S.I, DEA and maybe the F.B.I so with him we have to keep our hands clean. That's why Tim. We have to be on point. No mistakes. This officer thinks he's gonna get $40,000 out of me. We are going to play to his fantasies. Then blackball him. Chad, you and Lorenzo will take care of Sunnie and Tim, I want you to follow Mr. Officer to keep up with his whereabouts. Our message is when you fuck with us *you die.*"

*****

"Sunnie, what is Sammy going to do about that nigga in Queens?" asked Mike.

Sunnie smoked his cigar and looked in his hand at the three kings and two queens and said, "That's already taken care of." Then he threw $200 more on the poker table and said, "I'm raising the stakes $200." He leaned back in his chair and smiled. Jimmie looked at his hand and threw it down and said, "I fold."

"Me too," said Mike.

They all looked at Kevin. Kevin put $200 on the table and said, "Call your $200 and raise you $500." Looking dead in Sunnie's face.

"I call your bet.", Sunnie laid his hand down. He had a full house. "Kings over queens," said Sunnie as he smoked his cigar.

Kevin smiled back at him as he laid his hand out card by card. Ace, king, queen, jack, ten all the same suit. He smiled and said, "royal flush. Maybe next time Sunnie."

When he reached for the money, Sunnie took his knife out and stabbed him in his right hand. Kevin screamed. Mike jumped up and put a wire around his neck and was choking him. Kevin's face was turning blue.

Sunnie looked at him and said, "I hate a fucking cheater. How do you have a royal flush with the king of diamonds, when I have the king of diamonds in my hand?" said Sunnie.

Kevin was looking at him. Sunnie was angered. He pulled his knife out his hand and slit Kevin's throat pushing his body to the floor.

"Game over." said Sunnie as he walked to the bar and got a double shot of vodka. He looked at them and said, "get rid of the body."

It was 1 a.m. when Sunnie, Mike, and Jimmy walked out the bar. It was a chill breeze. Jimmy lowered his head to light a smoke. "Lorenzo you see them?"

"Yea, you ready?" asked Lorenzo.

"Remember, I need Sunnie alive."

When they pulled up, Lorenzo jumped out the van and put his .45 to Sunnie's head. Chad smacked Mike in the back of the head with a Billy club dropping him. Jimmy pulled his gun out and Lorenzo shot him dead in the chest and looked at Sunnie and said, "Fuck up and die too."

Sunnie looked at Jimmy's body drop and looked at Lorenzo and said, "What the fuck you want?" Lorenzo looked at him and smacked him in the face with the gun, knocking him out cold. They put their bodies in the van and tied them up.

"What about him?" said Chad looking at Jimmy's body.

"Put him in the van too," said Lorenzo.

Lorenzo called Jamila and said, "We got them."

"Bring them to the farm and I'll be down there in twenty minutes." She hung up her phone and walked out her office with Shawn and Tim behind her. No one said a word the whole car ride to the farm. Lorenzo saw the dim blue lights to the BMW coming down the dirt road. When the car came to a stop, Lorenzo walked up and opened the door for Jamila to get out.

"Where are they?" Jamila asked.

"The dead one is over there next to the tree," Lorenzo pointed to and I have the other two tied up in the van still.

Jamila looked at Shawn and Chad and said, "Bring them to me. And Nick, you and Tim strip him and tie him up to the tree over there. I want his body standing up."

Shawn pushed Sunnie down in front of Jamila. As he fell to his knees, Chad did the same thing with Mike. They looked up at Jamila with the headlights blinding them. Sunnie looked around and all he saw was trees and the black sky and Jamila standing in front of him.

Jamila looked at Lorenzo and said, "Tie this one next to his buddy on that tree."

Mike tried to fight again until Chad smacked him in the back of the head again, taking the fight out of him. Sunnie looked at Jamila and said, "What the fuck you want from me?"

She looked at him and said, "I don't have shit to say to you. I'll let you watch our conversation. Me and the one tied to the tree."

Jamila walked over to Mike and said, "Do you who I am?"

He looked at her and said, A dead nigga."

Jamila looked at him and said, "Tony, Joey and Bull said the same thing before they died. Now look at you trying to be brave."

She pulled her butterfly knife out and stabbed him in the face and said, "You're gonna die first, bitch."

Mike let out a scream, Jamila looked at him screaming. "You think I give a fuck about your pain or life? Fabio died because of y'all. Pussy."

She looked at Chad and said, "give me the crowbar." She handed him the knife and took the crowbar. Mike looked dead at her as she smacked him in the ribs as hard as she could breaking one of them.

Sunnie looked at him screaming out in pain. He tried to turn his head, but Lorenzo held his head still making him watch everything as Jamila beat him over and over again.

"I'm still a dead nigga?" she asked him. "What, you can't talk? You know how I feel? Let me tell you fuck the Lenacci Family, fuck Sammy, fuck Alex and fuck Sunnie. I'm playing for keeps."

Jamila smacked him in the face, knocking his teeth and blood out his mouth. She looked at Shawn and said, "strip him down. I want everything off."

She walked over to Sunnie and said, "give me his wallet." He handed it to her. She opened it and said, "Bingo." She walked back over to Mike as he looked at her and she took her knife and stabbed him in the heart and said, "tie him up in the barn. We will deal with him tomorrow." She handed his wallet to Chad and said, "you see this picture? Here is the address. Have them both here tomorrow no later than 2 p.m." He took the wallet and said, "Ok."

She looked at Lorenzo and said, "I'll see you tomorrow. Keep their bodies on the trees. Let's give the wild dogs something to eat tonight."

She walked back to the car and Shawn opened the door for her. She watched as Lorenzo dragged Sunnie in the barn as he was screaming and trying to fight them off with his hands tied behind his back. Tim backed the car up and Jamila said, "take me home. Shawn, I saw the way you looked at me when I was beating him. Hear me very well Muthafuckers only respect violence. Kill or be killed. Remember that."

Jamila grabbed his hand and said, "I don't have to second guess you, do I?"

"I'm loyal to this family. No, you don't I'm with you one hundred percent."

She nodded her head. Jamila ain't say nothing else the rest of the car ride.

Chapter Thirty-Seven

Present Day...

Frankie looked at Jamila and saw a demon in an angel's body. She had no remorse for the way she killed Sunnie and having Jimmy and Mike tied to a tree to be half eaten by wild dogs. She never talked about her next move, but her eyes talked, and they said more deaths and bodies to come.

"Jamila, how do you think this is going to end?" Asked Frankie.

Jamila cut her eyes at Frankie. "With me or Sammy in a casket. But one of us is going to die."

"And what do you think is going to happen when Sunnie doesn't show up in the next few days?"

"At this point I don't care. I want Sammy to come at me like a wild dog."

"And what do we do with mad dogs?"

"We put them to sleep".

"If Sammy had caught me slipping what you think he would have done to me? Shot me in the head? Beat me to death? What would he had done to me Frankie?"

"I don't know Jamila."

Frankie knew she was right. "I have more men under my belt, Frankie. An empire. I'm just getting off the ground, people I have to meet to sell the rest of the cocaine too. I have the most powerful mafia family in NYC who wants me dead. So, I got close to his boss and rolled him. Losing is not an opinion for me."

When the limousine pulled up at the restaurant, Chad opened the doors for Frankie and Marcus to get out. Frankie looked back at Jamila and said, "you know how to reach me if you need me."

"I do Frankie and thank you for having my back," said Jamila. Chad got back in the limo and Frankie watched as it pulled off.

*****

"Sammy, you have a Mr. Deniro here to see you." Sammy took his tongue and rubbed it across his front teeth and said, "send him in."

Deniro walked in the back office with a cane in his hand. Sammy was sitting down when he walked in.

"Sammy," Deniro said as he put his hand out to shake Sammy's hand.

"So, tell me Deniro. What do I owe the honor of this visit?" Said Sammy.

"Well, last night one of my guys was downtown Manhattan and he said it was a shooting. Three guys jumped out of a van and got Sunnie and the guys he was with. One of them I think was dead when they put them in the van."

Sammy got up and placed his hands on the desk and said, "What time was this?"

Deniro replied, "between 12 and 1 am. I recognized one of the guys."

Sammy walked to the front of his desk and said, "Who was the guy you recognized?"

"The fat one named Chad. He used to run with the Scott family. Now word is that this female Jamila has him working for her now," replied Deniro.

Sammy looked at Alex and said, "Call Sunnie." He then looked back at Deniro and said, "if what your man is saying is true, Sunnie is dead by now, Alex." Sammy called.

"Yea, Sammy I called a few times. He didn't pick up. I know he goes downtown with Jimmy, so I called Jimmy a few times. He didn't pick up."

"Fuck," said Sammy smacking his hand on the desk. "Deniro, can you give me any information on this Chad?" asked Sammy.

"Already done." Deniro handed him a piece of paper and got up and said, "Sometimes it's not the enemy you have to watch, but the company they keep with them." Deniro walked out of Sammy's office.

Sammy walked over to Alex and handed him the piece of paper and said, "have him killed tonight now." Alex got up and walked out the office.

SAYNOMORE

Chapter Thirty-Eight

Chad opened Jamila's limo door and walked her in the house.
"Are you good Mrs. LaCross? "asked Chad.
"Yes, Chad and thank you for all that you are doing for this family. I see all that you are doing for us."
"No, Jamila, thank you for giving me a home again."
Jamila gave Chad a hug and said, "be at the restaurant tomorrow at 1p.m.."
"I'll be there," said Chad. He walked out to his 2003 Jeep and placed his gun on the passenger seat and drove off. He made a right on Smith street and stopped at the red light. He looked around when the light turned green, he drove off. After making a few turns he took the left on his street. Before he could make it to his house, a car cut him off. Then a van pulled up behind him; he reached for his gun, but it was too late. Alex was standing in front of him with a M16 and four guys with high powered rifles. All you heard was the sounds of the guns going off. The driver's door opened up and Chad's body fell out. Alex walked over to his body and started shooting him at point blank range until his clip was empty. Chad's body was lying in a pool of blood, his own blood. You heard the sounds of car tires peeling out to get away and some watching the whole thing. Chad's body was still tweaking, he never had a chance.

*****

Lorenzo was at the bar eating his breakfast sandwich watching the news. When he saw the crime scene and the Jeep, he knew it was Chad who got killed. The witness said it was a black car and a blue van that pulled up and cut him off and started shooting. Since the war with the Lenacci family began, Isaiah, Nayana, Fabio, Tesfar, Cordial, Chad, Abby and Elisha's families were gone. Bodies were dropping left and right. They needed to kill Sammy and end this war, but it was like he knew their every move.

He walked upstairs to Jamila's office and was setting everything up for the meeting today. He was also thinking about how he was going to tell Jamila about Chad's killing. When Jamila walked in her office, she laid her bags on the table and saw the look on Lorenzo's face.

"What happened now Lorenzo?" asked Jamila.

"Last night Chad got killed. I saw his Jeep on the news and the crime scene. It was ugly. They did a number on him."

Jamila looked at him and said, "have someone claim the body, and take care of the funeral. He was part of this family and we take care of ours and find out who did this."

"Who else Jamila? It was Sammy," said Lorenzo.

"Ok Lorenzo," said Jamila. "We have to deal with what we have going on today. We have four meetings. Once we get them out the way then we will deal with Sammy and this cop character."

Lorenzo walked up to the table and dropped the duffle bag on it and said, "everything you asked me to bring is in there. I'll go make sure everyone is at their post."

Jamila looked at the bag and said, "Thank you."

"You know I got your back," said Lorenzo before walking out.

Jamila looked in the bag at the kilos of cocaine and at her stamp on them. She placed the bag in the closet. She knew Dapp was coming for ten of them today and a few other people as well. She couldn't get Chad's killing out her head knowing he grew on her. She remembered his last words to her. Jamila knew Sammy was the rabbit and she was the turtle in this race. She had to keep going and outthink him. Frankie asked her how this was going to end, and she said with one of us dead. She knew Sammy wasn't going to leave his bar or be out in the open at all. So, she would have to go to him. That's the only way to kill him. She was going to have to go to his front door.

Jamila picked up the phone and called Frankie. When he picked up, he sounded sleepy. "Hello."

"Hey, I'm sorry if I woke you up but, I need a favor."

"What can I do for you Jamila?" asked Frankie

"I need a few men tomorrow before 12 p.m."

"May I ask for what?" said Frankie.

144

"Frankie, I'm sure they will let you know all the details tomorrow," replied Jamila.

"Ok Jamila. Where do you want them to meet you at?" asked Frankie.

"My house will be fine."

"They will be there, and you know you have one shot with the Lenacci family," said Frankie.

"I know, and Frankie make sure they are heavily armed."

"They will be," replied Frankie.

Jamila hung up the phone and took out her 9mm and placed it in the top desk drawer. It was already 11:45 p.m. and a Mr. Johnson was supposed to be there by 12 p.m. Fabio had him in his book with five stars by his name. From the phone conversation, Jamila knew he was about his business. Jamila walked over to her bar in her office and took out a bottle of grape water. That's when she heard a knock at the door. When she opened it, it was Lorenzo and Mr. Johnson.

"Hello Mr. Johnson please come in." Lorenzo nodded his head and walked back downstairs.

"Mr. Johnson. Can I get you something to drink water or something stronger?" asked Jamila.

"Water would be just fine Ms. LaCross."

"Please call me Jamila."

"So, Jamila, Fabio never talked about you," said Mr. Johnson.

"There are a lot of things Fabio never talked about, but here we both are and hopefully we can continue to do business Mr. Johnson," said Jamila.

"Please call me Derrick."

"So, shall we get down to business Ms. LaCross?" Mr. Johnson said as he opened his bottle of water.

"All the prices are the same as they have been and all the product is the same grade A as it was before," said Jamila.

"Is there a sample I can test?" asked Derrick

"Sure, there is, and you said to me you wanted the same as, always right?"

"That is correct Jamila."

Jamila got up and walked to the closet and pulled out a bag and walked to the table and pulled out two kilos of cocaine and placed it on the table.

"Here are your samples," said Jamila.

Derrick looked at both kilos and pulled out his pocket a small clear glass bottle with a liquid in it. He cut the kilos open just enough to take a sample out. Then he placed it in the bottle and in a few seconds the liquid turned blue. He did these two more times to make sure.

Jamila just watched him. He looked at her and pulled out an envelope out his top right pocket with $50,000 in it and handed it to her. She looked at it and placed it down on the table. Derrick looked at her and said, "Jamila it was nice doing business with you."

"Likewise, Mr. Johnson. So, when shall I see you again?" Asked Jamila.

"Within thirty days," said Mr. Johnson as he picked up his bag and Jamila walked him out to the front lobby.

Before 3 p.m. came, Jamila saw Dapp and everyone else she made a gross of $400,000. She put the money in a safe and picked up her gun and walked downstairs to the main floor. She walked up to Tim and said, "Go get the car. We need to take a ride somewhere."

"Just the two of us?" asked Tim.

"Yes and bring the black BMW." said Jamila

"Yes Ms. LaCross."

Lorenzo walked over to her when he saw her in the lobby. "Hey, where are you about to go?"

"To go double check Sammy's address and if I'm right about this, tomorrow morning we have a job to go do." Said Jamila.

"Hold on I'm coming with you Jamila," said Lorenzo.

"No," said Jamila. "I need you here. I'll be fine, trust me Lorenzo. I'm on point."

That's when Tim pulled up front with the car. Lorenzo and Nick walked Jamila outside.

"So where are we going Ms. LaCross?"

"To this address." Jamila handed him a piece of paper and leaned back in her seat and said, "Tim when you get to the street pull over somewhere, but not in front of the house, but close enough to see how many cars are there and men outside."

"Yes, ma'am."

SAYNOMORE

Chapter Thirty-Nine

Sammy was outside talking to Alex in the front of the house.

"So, what now Sammy?" Asked Alex.

"We know by now Sunnie is dead, so I need you to take his place and be my number two guy. We lost a lot of good men in this war, but they will not die alone. Tony's death hurt us all, but just like Fabio's mother and father, his ass is dead too. And soon Jamila will die too." Said Sammy

"You know Sammy, word came to me yesterday that she is supplying Queens right now. Did Omar ever get back to you on that?" Asked Alex.

"I'm waiting to hear something now, but what I do know, Alex is we have a snake amongst us. Someone is helping Jamila out. Ain't no way she knows our whereabouts. What we need to do is find out who's helping her and feed them to the fishes."

"Sammy, you want me to put a few guys on the restaurant to see who's coming in and out of there." Said Alex.

"You know what Alex, do that. I want to know everyone she is doing business with. Take pictures."

*****

Jamila's car rode past Sammy and Alex as they were talking. None of them paid attention when the black BMW parked a few houses up. They were there for twenty-five minutes watching them. That's when Jamila saw a navy-blue GMC Yukon SLT SUV pull up and Alex walked to the truck and got in. Sammy and a few other men walked back in the house.

"Tim, follow that truck. I want to see where he is going," said Jamila.

They followed the truck all the way Downtown Manhattan to the same bar Sunnie was at. That's when Alex got out and the driver of the truck drove off.

"Ms. LaCross, do you want me to follow the truck still?" Said Tim.

"Yea, I want to talk to the driver of that truck." said Jamila
They followed the truck until it pulled in a parking space.

"Tim let me out," said Jamila. "Listen, pull up next to his truck
and when he gets out, put the gun to his head. I'll come from this
way just in case," said Jamila. Tim nodded his head and pulled off.

Jamila had her gun in her hand as she walked up to the truck.
When the door opened, the driver didn't see Tim walk up behind
him. That's when he heard the clicking of a gun being cocked back.
When he turned around, Tim had the gun to his head.

"Fuck up and die. Hands where I can see them." Tim walked up
to him and patted him down, taking his gun off of him.

"What the fuck you want?"

Jamila walked up and said, "he doesn't want anything. I want
to talk with you."

He looked at her and said, "you must be Jamila. I've been
hearing so much about you."

"So, you want to talk here, or would you like to go somewhere
else and talk?" asked Jamila.

He looked around and said, "here," knowing everyone who's
been killed by her. He ain't want to take no chances. "First things
first," Jamila said. "Give me your wallet."

He reached in his pocket and pulled it out and handed it to her.

"So, is that where I'm going to die at?"

"That's up to you," said Jamila as she looked in his wallet and
said, "Anthony. I don't want to kill you, but I will if I have to."

"So, what do you want from me?", said Anthony.

"This is how this is going to go."

Anthony looked at Tim holding the gun to his head knowing
he will kill him at the drop of a dime.

Jamila said, "I just want a simple yes or no. You understand
me.?

"Yea, I do," said Anthony.

"Are you Alex's driver?" asked Jamila

"Yes."

"Are you picking him back up tonight?"

"No."

"What time do you pick him up in the morning?" said Jamila.

"It depends between 9 and 10 am," said Anthony.

"Then where do you go?'

"Sammy's house then we leave there by 12 noon to head to the bar."

Jamila looked at his family pictures and said, "This must be your son and daughter. And this beautiful lady must be your wife." Jamila looked at his expression on his face and said, "Don't say nothing stupid. This is what I need, and you are going to help me, you understand?"

"Yes," said Anthony.

"Tomorrow morning after you leave Sammy's house, you are going to make sure Alex is by himself. And you're not going to do shit when we kidnap him. If you try to help him, I swear I'll kill everyone in your fucking family and make you watch. You have my word I'm not going to kill him or hurt him. I just want to talk to him. And if you play ball you will never see me again. Can you do that for me Anthony?" said Jamila.

"If they think I had anything to do with it, they will kill me," said Anthony.

"Don't worry about that they won't. So you got me?" said Jamila.

Anthony nodded his head. "Yes"

"Let's go." Jamila walked past Anthony and said, "you have a nice night and I'll keep this ID for insurance. Please don't make me put innocent blood on my hands."

Tim opened the car door and Jamila got in. "All she wanted to do was talk," he said as he got in the car and drove off.

SAYNOMORE

Chapter Forty

Frankie's men met with Jamila at nine that morning and she went over all the details with them.

Jamila and Lorenzo sat in a limousine a few blocks over. Frankie's men were in place. As Sammy's gates opened, they watched Alex and his driver pull out. As they made it to the end of the street, the first van pulled out in front of them and the side door opened, and two men jumped out holding AR-15s and pointed at them. The driver tried to back up, but the second van pulled up behind them and another guy jumped out with a M16 and pointed at them. One of the guys walked up to Alex's door and opened it.

"Don't get killed," he told Alex. "Someone wants to talk with you. So, you can either die here or live another day."

Alex got out of the car after looking at his driver. He got patted down and took his gun off of him. They placed a paper bag over his head and put him in the van. Then you heard three shots and the van pulled off. Alex knew they just killed his driver. They drove a little way and pulled over.

"Get out and watch your step. Follow my voice." As they put Alex in the limousine, one of Frankie's men sat next to him. Jamila pulled the paper bag off of Alex's head and said, "Hello Alex. How are you doing today? Don't worry, I'm not going to kill you no matter how many bitches you called me."

Alex looked at Jamila. She had on a red dress with a slit going up the side with a black dog chain on it with a pair of stilettos on. Her hair was curled down. She had on blood red lipstick.

"So, let me get this right. You kidnapped me just to tell me you ain't going to kill me?" he asked. "So, what do you want."

"I want you to know your life is in my hands. It was just that easy to find out where you were at and now look, you are here with me. You do remember my associate Lorenzo? You shot him in the shoulder." Lorenzo looked at him with death in his eyes.

"Alex, I don't give a fuck how powerful the Lenacci family is or used to be because right now, you are dropping like flies. I can kill you right now and drop your body off in the woods somewhere and I won't lose a night of sleep. I want you to hear me and hear me very fucking well. Sammy killed my friends, family and my fiancée and you tried to kill me and my associate," said Jamila. "This is the only time I will tell you this. I will kill every fucking Lenacci there is so, if Sammy even thinks about coming at me again," Jamila leaned in closer to Alex and said, "he better think twice, his balls are in my fucking hands. And when I kill a fucking Lenacci, they are my stress relievers."

Lorenzo just looked at him as Jamila talked. Then he said, "This is the new Queen of Queens and before anybody comes to Queens to do anything, they will get her permission first. Or we will take it as a sign of disrespect and bodies will come up missing. Do I make myself clear?" said Lorenzo.

Jamila said, "Alex to show you I'm not playing, take a look at these pictures." Jamila showed him everyone she had killed, tied up to a tree, burned alive. Then she showed him Tony's still tied up to a chair with his dick hanging out. She watched his face expression and said, "Does that hurt your feelings looking at Tony before he got his throat cut from ear to ear?" said Jamila

"Alex you see your friends are dying. Be smart and don't join them." Alex's face was red looking at all the pictures of them. "Alex I can get at anyone I fucking want too. So, don't forget it, and one more thing. If you need me or want to get in touch with me, here's a phone you can call me on. This is the only line I will pick up on. Now, you can see your way out of my limo."

Jamila tapped the glass and the limo pulled over letting Alex out. Then pulled off.

"Jamila, do you think it was wise for you to do that?" said Lorenzo.

"Lorenzo, I just put the ball in his court. As for you Marcus, I want to thank you for your help today. I will make sure Frankie knows how much you helped me out today." Said Jamila.

"You are welcome. You can let me out here," said Marcus.

"Are you sure?" asked Jamila

"Yes, my guys have been following behind us to make sure nothing happened."

Jamila knew she had to dot all of her I's and cross all of her T's. She had the driver pull over and let Marcus out. Once the limo pulled off, she said, "Lorenzo, you are my number two, but don't ever question me in front of no one ever again."

When Marcus reached Frankie's house, Frankie looked at him and asked, "What did she need you for?"

"Frankie, one thing I can say about her is every move she makes is like a game of chess to her. She plans all the way to the end. She is playing the role of a true boss and knows how to move like one."

Frankie looked at Marcus and said, "Again, what did she need you for? What did you do?"

"You ready for this one? We kidnapped Alex," said Marcus.

Frankie looked at Marcus and said, "Wait did I hear you right?"

"Yea, you did," replied Marcus. "She set it up the way she wanted it to go down."

"So, Marcus what happened?" asked Frankie.

"We went to Sammy's house."

"Marcus, you went to Sammy's house?"

"Yea, I told you she moves like a boss. We waited twenty minutes. She told us what time he would be pulling out. She told us the color of the car and how many people would be in the car. And she was right. When the car made it up the street, we blocked him off and snatched him up and brought him to her," said Marcus.

"So where did she have you dump the body at?" asked Frankie.

"She ain't want him dead. She talked to him for a few minutes, told him what she wanted Sammy to know. showed him some pictures of dead Lenacci members then she kicked him out the limo."

"Marcus did he see your face?" Asked Frankie

"No, I had a mask on the whole time. She had perfect timing on everything."

Frankie looked at him and said, "She mastered the art of timing."

"So, she didn't do anything to him?"

"Not one thing," said Marcus.

"Marcus, let me ask you what you think of her?"

"Truthfully, if she wasn't an ally, she would be a big threat."

*****

"So, you are telling me this little black bitch killed Tony?" said Sammy.

"Sammy, I saw the pictures of him tied to a chair still alive. She could have killed me, but she didn't. Look at what they did to my driver. They shot him three times. He's lucky to still be alive. I'm still alive. So, can I tell you a message," said Alex.

"And what's the message she wanted you to tell me?" Said Sammy.

"She said your balls are in her hands and you have one more time to come after her and she will kill everyone in the Lenacci family," stated Alex.

Sammy looked at Alex and said, "she will be dead in two weeks. Find out where she stays at. I want her head on my fucking table yesterday. Who the fuck she thinks she is? And how did she find out where I stay?"

"Sunnie told her. She beat him and beat him until he told her what she wanted to know. Sammy, I looked in her eyes. She's heartless," said Alex.

"Alex, get a new driver and take care of what I asked you to do."

Chapter Forty-One

"Mr. Frankie, you have a visitor. A Mr. Scott is here to see you," said Ms. Simpson.

Frankie walked from the back room to the front and shook his hand.

"So, Frankie," said Mr. Scott. "It's been a long time."

"Yea, it has been Jason. So, tell me what brings you by?" Asked Frankie.

"Is there somewhere we can talk?" Asked Jason.

"Sure, come out back to the pool. Ms. Simpson, please bring us some drinks outside," said Frankie.

"Yes, Sir."

"So, Jason," said Frankie, "what is it you wanted to talk to me about?"

"Frankie, we have been friends for a long time. Over twenty years and I know how close you were to Fabio. By taking him under your wing when his parents got killed." Frankie looked at him while he was talking and lit his cigar. "And I know Fabio's death hurt you."

Frankie cut him off. "With the utmost respect Jason Where is this going?" At that time Ms. Simpson brought them two glasses of Brandy outside with two ice cubes in them.

"I'm not slow Frankie. Everyone else might not have put it together but I already did," said Jason. "I know you know who this Jamila is and from what I'm seeing and hearing, she is no one to play with."

"And why do you think I know who she is, Jason?" said Frankie.

"Because word is, she was Fabio's soon to be wife. Now she owns Jelani's and is moving weight in Queens. So, I know you know who she is."

"Jason," said Frankie, "there was a dog, and all the neighbors came together to feed this dog. And no matter how many times they fed this dog, he kept knocking over trash cans. Making a mess and marking his territory, yet he still wanted to eat and eat. A new neighbor moved in the neighborhood and this dog knocked over their trash can too."

"So, what did ya do to stop the dog from knocking over the trash can?" asked Jason.

"Well, the neighbors tried to talk to the new neighbor and said, 'we can just feed the dog more.' Well, the owners of the trash can say, well sometimes you can't feed a dog. You just have to put him to sleep."

Jason picked up his glass and took a sip and said, "I understand."

"And Jason my hands are clean of everything. I'm just watching the show," said Frankie.

"Frankie again, I've known you for a very long time and I have no reason to question your loyalty to the rules of the game we all play," said Jason. "Frankie, I would like to meet this neighbor. Can you set that up?"

"I think I may be able to do that today or maybe tomorrow morning. What would be good for you?" asked Frankie.

"Tomorrow morning would be just fine."

Mr. Scott got up and shook Frankie's hand and said, "I'll see you tomorrow morning no later than 9 a.m."

"I'll see you then," said Frankie. Frankie watched as he walked off. Ms. Simpson walked to the table and picked up the glass and Frankie told her to bring the phone. Within a few minutes, Frankie was on the phone with Jamila and told her to have extra security there tomorrow morning. He was bringing somebody to meet her in the morning at nine.

*****

Sammy was at the bar playing pool smoking his cigar and talking shit about Jamila. When he saw Jason walk in, he laid his pool stick down on the pool table and told his guys hold on and that he needed to talk with him. Sammy smacked his hands together and smiled saying, "Jason so tell me what you have to tell me. Have a seat. Have a seat," said Sammy.

"I got everything you asked for right here." Jason pulled out a tape recorder and pressed play. Sammy listened in silence at every word Frankie said. After fifteen minutes Sammy said, "So do you think he's lying?"

"Sammy, I've known Frankie for over twenty years. I have always known him to be truthful, even when Fabio's parents were killed. He raised that boy as his own, but still he never went against the Lenacci family. He knows her, but I'm not going to believe he is helping her at all. But only tomorrow when I meet her will I know the truth. And from what I got from his story, he said in so many words he told her to pay dues like everyone else, but she refused."

Sammy said, "when you see her tomorrow find out everything you can for me."

"Sammy, I'm not going to have this tape recorder on me tomorrow. Nine times out of ten, I'll get patted down," said Jason.

"Yea, you might be right. Just find out what you can for me," said Sammy.

"I will."

Sammy patted Jason on the back and went back to his pool game.

SAYNOMORE

Chapter Forty-Two

Jamila had two men at the door and three men walking the restaurant floor. She had Nick, Tim, and Shawn in her office with her. When Frankie walked inside Jelani's with Jason and looked around, he saw Lorenzo walking up to him, he shook both of their hands.

"Frankie, it's nice to see you," said Lorenzo.

"Likewise, Lorenzo. This is Jason Scott of the Scott Family. And this is Lorenzo of the LaCross family. I have an appointment with Jamila this morning," Said Frankie.

"Ok," replied Lorenzo. "I'll see you both upstairs." Lorenzo called one of the security guards over and had him pat Frankie and Jason down. He took both of their weapons and placed them in a lock box. When they reached the second range as they stepped off the elevator, Jason looked at the men she had standing at her office door. Before they walked in her office, they got patted down again. Jamila was walking from her birdcage when she saw Lorenzo, Frankie and Jason walk in her office. Nick also walked in and was standing by the office door. Jason looked at how beautiful she was. She was nothing like he imagined from her long hair to her hazel eyes to the hourglass figure. Jamila walked up to Frankie and gave him a kiss on the cheeks.

"Jamila, this is Jason Scott of the Scott family. And Jason, this is Jamila LaCross of the LaCross family," said Frankie.

He extended his hand to her.

"Nice to meet you Jamila."

"You too Jason."

"Frankie, you look like you could eat something. Lorenzo, can you take Frankie downstairs and have the chef make him some breakfast while me and Mr. Scott talk, "said Jamila.

Frankie got up and walked with Lorenzo out the office. When the doors closed, Jamila looked at Jason and said, "Can I get you something to drink? Water, wine or something stronger?"

"No thanks, I'm fine." said Jason.

"So, Jason," asked Jamila, "What can I do for you?"

"I really just wanted to meet you. I heard so much about you. So, I wanted to meet the woman everyone is talking about." Said Jason.

"So, who is everyone Jason?" asked Jamila

"All the families."

Jamila looked at him as he was talking. "So, what about Mr. Sammy? How does he feels about me?" asked Jamila.

Jason cut his eyes as he looked away and said, "he wants to end this war from what I'm told."

Jamila got up and walked to the glass doors and said, "You know what Jason, when I first got this restaurant from Fabio, I looked out this very door and looked down and said, this is a long fall down if someone was to fall over the edge," she turned around and walked back to the edge of the table Jason was sitting at. "See, I find it very funny that you wanted to meet me out of nowhere. But I played with the idea for a little and said, what the hell I'll meet him. And Jason, you failed the test," said Jamila. "Within the first ten minutes you refused a drink from me that was strike one. The second one was when I asked you about Sammy and you said, he wanted to end this war with me. But see when you cut your eyes and refused to look at me, I knew you were lying.

"Let's see where the third strikes are. We are going to play a game called Truth or Death. I'll ask you some questions and I want a simple answer. If you lie, you die. It's that simple. Let's play Jason," said Jamila.

First question, "Did Sammy have you come talk to me?" Jason looked at her and knew she would have him killed if she thought he was lying to her.

"Yes, he did." replied Jason.

Jamila looked at him and said, "I don't care why he wanted you to meet me. But I do need you to give him something for me. Can you do that Jason?" asked Jamila

"If you don't mind." She got up and walked to her desk and came back with a little box and three roses and said, "let him know the white rose is for the innocent lives that's been killed. The red rose is for the blood that was spilled. And the black rose is for his death. And for the record, Jason. I have no problems with you or anybody else and make sure you give him this black box too for me."

Jason took the box and rose, and Jamila said, "Now you have a nice day Mr. Scott. Nick, can you see Mr. Scott to his car or Mr. Landon? And Jason, Frankie trusted you. You can tell him, or I can tell him the real reason you visited his house yesterday."

Jason walked out the doors to the lobby. Frankie was talking with Lorenzo still eating when he saw Jason coming his way.

"Are you ready?" Frankie asked Jason.

"Yea, I am." replied Jason.

Lorenzo had both of their weapons returned with the clips out of them and he walked them to the door to see them out.

*****

Omar sat in the chair with blood coming from his head. His hands were tied up with chains so were his feet. His shoes were off and so was his shirt. He looked around and all he saw was a wet floor and barrels of water. He remembered walking in his house then getting hit over the head with something that was last night. He heard someone talking when he looked up, he saw two men walking his way.

"I see you are up now. You've been asleep for eight hours."

"Where am I?" Omar asked.

"Don't worry. Someone will be here to talk with you soon enough, to answer all your questions."

At that point, he knew it was Jamila who got him.

"How long before she comes?" asked Omar.

"She is not coming to see you. Someone else is." That's when a bright light hit him in the face as the warehouse doors were opening up. He saw a man walking his way. Lorenzo put a chair in front of him and said, "I'm sorry we had to meet this way. You were very hard to follow. Two days of following you and you led us to your house. Now we are here."

Lorenzo took his gun and laid it on the table with a chainsaw and over fifteen knives. Omar looked at the table and said, "Am I supposed to be scared?"

"I hope not," said Lorenzo.

"So, if you are going to kill me let's get it over with."

"Jamila doesn't want you dead at all, but before I let you hurt her or kill her, I will put you six feet deep."

Omar started laughing out loud. "You think because I'm in chains, that I'm scared.? Do you know who the fuck I am?" said Omar. "I have the Lenacci family watching my back. I have half of the NYPD ready to kill for me. So, fuck you, fuck Jamila and fuck what you stand on. I'm Omar Reeds muthafucker."

Lorenzo picked his gun up and said, "you are right Mr. Reeds," and walked away. That's when Honduras walked up with a pair of black rubber gloves on and a black apron on with a black face mask. He took one of the knives off the table and walked up to Omar. Omar looked him dead in the eyes with no sign of fear. Honduras took the knife and cut Omar's nipple off. Omar let out a scream. He cut Omar across the chest. Omar was shaking and yelling. He cut him all over his body so all you heard was Omar screaming and yelling throughout the warehouse is his voice echoing off the walls. He passed out because of loss of blood and pain. Before it was all over, there was more blood than water on the floor and Omar's lifeless body was leaning over in the chair still.

Jamila watched the whole thing from the corner of the warehouse. Nick walked up to her and she said, "have his body dumped behind the bar in the dumpster downtown Manhattan and make sure ya clean this place up. I don't want no DNA on the floor." After she said that, she turned to Tim and said, "take me to the restaurant," as she walked off.

Chapter Forty-Three

Before they could make it to the restaurant, the streets were blocked off. You had NYPD and FDNY out there and people standing around watching the whole thing. Jelani's was on fire in a deadly blaze. You saw smoke in flames coming from the windows. You had three fire trucks fighting down the fire, and policemen keeping the crowd back. Jamila got out of the car and was looking at her restaurant being burned down. She got back in the car and told Tim to get her out of there. She called Lorenzo and told him what happened, and she needed him to get down there ASAP.

"Ms. LaCross is there any place you want to go?" asked Tim.

"Head down 145th I'll tell you where we are going in a few." Jamila looked down at her phone. That's when a car side swiped them and ran them off the road, causing them to hit a tree. Jamila's head went through the window, breaking the glass, making her dizzy. Tim's head hit the steering wheel making a big gash above his eyebrow. When he looked up, he saw a black SUV with two guns aimed at them out the window. Before he could say anything, they opened fire on the car hitting him in the chest, arm and shoulder. Jamila got shot in her back and shoulder. Tim put the car in reverse and tried to back up. Jamila was leaning over trying to catch her breath.

"Jamila, Jamila. Can you hear me?" said Tim as he looked back and saw she was shot. He was going 95 mph trying to get away. When he lost consciousness from the loss of blood, he hit a parked car flipping the car over on its back. The impact of the hit threw Jamila out the car over into someone's yard. Her body was just lying there. Tim was hanging out the window when the truck pulled up next to the car. He looked at them and saw the guns as they fired shots at his head before he died. Kenny looked at Jamila's body lying on the concrete. He opened up the door and Jimmy stopped him.

"She's dead. Look at her, Kenny. Let's get out of here now." Kenny closed the truck door and drove off.

*****

Jason sat there looking at Sammy as he paced the floor talking. "So, this white rose is for innocence. The red is for the blood that was spilled, and the black is for my death. Three roses and Omar's badge. What the fuck? He's dead too?" Looking at Jason he said, "So how is it there?" said Sammy.

Jason got up and said, "Sammy, she's got tight security from the men at the door to walking the floor. She had me and Frankie patted down twice before we could meet her. She is smart. She threatened me without saying."

"What do you mean?" asked Sammy.

"She walked up to the desk and said, it's a long fall down. Then she turned around and looked at me." Jason was drinking a glass of Brandy. He had his legs crossed leaning back in his chair.

"Sammy with the utmost respect, there's been more blood spilled in the last year then I could remember. Everyone is losing money and it's being talked about from the Deniro family, to my family, to the Landon family as well. This war is crossing over to Brooklyn, the Bronx, even Manhattan. We have police pressing down on us. We can't move like we need to right now. It's hot out there." Sammy's phone started to ring. He looked at his desk and headed that way to pick up the phone.

"Yea," he said into the phone receiver. "Ok, ok. Are you sure? Then good." Sammy hung up the phone and said, "Mr. Scott, my little problem is dead as of twenty minutes ago. And the restaurant is burned down. So, what were you saying again?" said Sammy.

Jason got up and said, "Problem solved then." He shook Sammy's hand and walked out the room. Jason walked out the bar once he was in his car, he called Frankie and told Frankie the news. He told his driver to take him to 125th. They saw Jelani's was set on fire and that the fire got the best of the restaurant. Everything was blocked off and they could feel the heat still coming from the building.

*****

Frankie saw the road was still blocked off, but he could see that Jelani's was set on fire. "Marcus, go around to 145th and we'll take the backroad back to the house." After ten minutes of driving he saw Jamila's car and Tim's bullet-ridden body halfway out of the car. "Stop Marcus, check to see if you see Jamila."

That's when Frankie saw her laid out on the ground. He ran over to her and checked to see if she was still alive. Marcus ran over there with him.

"Yea," Frankie said, "help me carry her to the car, hurry up."

Once in the car Frankie said, "get me to the house hurry up now. She lost a lot of blood. Jamila, hold on you are going to be alright, I promise," said Frankie.

As he held her in his arms, she opened her eyes and saw Frankie before passing back out again.

"Marcus, hurry up," yelled Frankie. When they pulled up to the house, Frankie and Marcus got Jamila to the back where she was taken care of. Frankie had blood all over him. He looked back at Marcus and said, "have someone go back there and see if they can find her phone and gun. We don't need the police finding it. The good part is that it's a private road so it ain't no traffic really on that road."

Marcus said, "Ok" and left. Frankie called Lorenzo and told him he needs to get to his house now. Then he went in the back where Jamila was at.

SAYNOMORE

Chapter Forty-Four

It had been five days since the fire and Jamila's shooting. Lorenzo and a rebuilder walked in what was left of Jelani's

"So, what are we talking about to get this place back to how it uses to be?" asked Lorenzo.

"It's going to be a few months. The good part is that the fire only hit the main floor. The bad part is the water damage but we're talking anywhere from $150,000 to $200,000 and about six to seven months of working.

"When can you start?" said Lorenzo. "And there is going to be a few changes."

After leaving the restaurant, he went to check on Jamila at Frankie's house. Jamila was outside, seated with her crutches beside her, looking at the pool when Lorenzo pulled up. She got up and gave him a hug and kiss.

"How you, Jamila?" asked Lorenzo

"I'm still a little sore, but I'm good," she replied. "What they say about the restaurant?"

Lorenzo sat down next to Jamila and said, "they are going to start working on it this week coming up."

"I need to get home and get things rolling," said Jamila.

"Jamila," said Lorenzo, "you just escaped death not even a week ago."

"Lorenzo now it's time that Sammy feels my pain." Jamila got up and said, "Take me to my house. This muthafucker is going to die now. How many men have we lost Lorenzo?" asked Jamila.

"I counted fourteen."

"How many of them were killed?"

"Eight."

"It's time we move smarter until Jelani's is up and running again. We are going to be taking care of all business out of a waste plant. I'm calling a meeting tonight. I want everyone at the waste plant by 6:30." Said Jamila.

Lorenzo shook his head looking at Jamila talking. Jamila walked in the house towards Frankie and said, "Thank you" to him.

Before she left, he gave her a kiss on the cheek and told her to be careful.

*****

Walking in the waste plant, Jamila saw everyone. She said, "Fabio is dead, Tesfar is dead. Cordial is dead, Chad, Tim, Nayana and Isaiah are all dead. I personally killed Cordial. I shot him point blank range in the face. And I personally killed Nayana. I shot her in the face as well because they both were disloyal."

Jamila walked around the table looking like a runway model. "I have trust in all of you, but I will be damned if I see another LaCross be put to rest. So, we are going to hit up Sammy's bar and house. I just found out where he's at tonight. He's at the strip club having a meeting. I don't give a fuck who he's having a meeting with. Everyone dies tonight. If they are standing with Sammy, they are the enemies. So, we got a bullet for they asses too. Lorenzo, you and Nick have Sammy's house. Elisha, you and Shawn have the bar. Honduras and I have the strip club. I want groups of four. Kill or be killed is how we are doing this tonight."

Jamila pulled up outside the strip club. It was 9:30pm that night. "Honduras, you and James walk in first. Nine times out of ten, Sammy's going to be in VIP with whoever. Me and Kent will be right behind you too. Once I come in the doors and you see me, stand up. All hell breaks loose. Ya understand?" said Jamila

"Yea."

Honduras walked in the club with James right beside him. They walked to a table in the back and took their seats. When Jamila walked in, she sat at the bar and Kent walked to the table right on the side of the VIP. Jamila was watching everything and everyone.

*****

"Sammy now that this ongoing war for a year is over, let's get back to business," said Mr. Washington.

"Good because I have someone already getting a spot ready in Queens." Said Sammy. "Now let's talk about the numbers."

"Sammy the numbers are negotiable, but the best I can do is $22,500 a kilo. Now, if you are buying thirty to forty a pop I can drop the prices down to $18,500," Mr. Washington said as he smoked his pipe.

"I can work with those prices," replied Sammy

"So, what's next for the Lenacci family Sammy?" asked Mr. Washington.

"I don't know yet," said Sammy. "Now that I have full control over Queens, I might open an underground casino. Run some numbers."

Jamila looked at Honduras then James and stood up. From the females that were dancing on stage to the ones doing lap dances. No one noticed that she had on a trench coat. She looked dead at Mr. Washington when he saw her, he told Sammy. He turned around and looked at her. That's when Kent looked at the bodyguards he had at the door and opened fire hitting one of them in the chest.

Then Jamila pulled out her Mac-11 and shot up the VIP. Honduras then pulled his shotgun out with James shooting everything by the VIP. Mr. Washington's men were shooting back. Jamila ran for cover. Sammy was standing behind the door shooting at them yelling, "Kill that bitch now." Mr. Washington was on the floor when his man grabbed him and was shooting their way out the back door taking him to safety. Honduras ran up and shot one of the bouncers in the face, killing him. Sammy saw his man's dead body hit the floor. It was so many people yelling and screaming trying to get out of there. Sammy took off running out the back door. That's when he got shot in the leg by Jamila. Once outside, he was hiding behind a dumpster. Jamila ran outside behind him and said, "Come the fuck outside, you fucking coward."

Sammy yelled back, "your niggas are hard to fucking kill." Then he jumped from behind the dumpster. Jamila saw him and shot at him as he ran behind a car and ducked behind it.

Jamila said, "Your men fucked up. They did everything but kill me."

"Don't worry, I'll get it done myself," yelled Sammy back at her.

That's when Honduras came out the door. Jamila pointed at the car. Sammy looked at his clip and saw he only had three rounds left. He turned around and saw a car pull up. Alex jumped out shooting at Jamila. Sammy took off running to the car. Jamila and Honduras were shooting at him as he reached the car. He got shot in the back and fell face down. Jamila ducked down behind the dumpster as Alex was shooting an M16 at her and Honduras. They got Sammy in the car and pulled off. Jamila watched as the car peeled off.

Honduras said, "we killed four of them inside. We need to go before the cops come."

Jamila walked back inside and saw all the bodies and said, "Let's go."

They left right as the police were pulling up.

Chapter Forty-Five

Lorenzo sat in a black SUV outside of Sammy's house. Looking at the men he had watching his grounds, he remembered seeing one of the bodyguards named Kenny, but didn't remember where.

"Nick, me and you will set the house on fire while you two wait out front with the M16. As soon as they try and run out the door, light their ass up," said Lorenzo. "Me and Nick will be around back just in case they try to get out the back door."

Lorenzo walked watching as they all went into the house. "Come on Now," said Lorenzo.

Within a few minutes the house was on fire. Lorenzo and Nick were in the back watching everything in the bushes.

"Kenny you smell that?"

"Smell what, Rock?"

That's when Kenny looked and saw the smoke coming from downstairs.

"Oh, shit Rock. The house is on fire," said Kenny. "We got to get out of here now."

Rock ran downstairs and opened the front door. That's when KO and Cali Boy started shooting at him. He dives back in and closed the door. He yells, "They are shooting at us from outside. What do we do now?" said Rock.

"How many?", said Kenny.

"I don't know."

Kenny started shooting back and said, "It's two of them out front. We can't go out that way." Smoke started to fog up the house.

"Rock stay down as low as you can. Where is Steve at?" said Kenny.

That's when they saw Steve dead on the floor. He got hit when they shot the house up.

"Kenny the back door. We can make it," said Rock.

"No, Rock. Don't go out the back door. Just stay down." The ceiling starts to fall in. Kenny was laying behind a desk KO yells, "Keep shooting. They got to come out of there."

The front door fell in, blocking the path out. Rock looked at Kenny one more time before he got up and ran out the back door. As he jumped off the porch, he got shot with a double barrel shotgun in the chest. The impact threw him back on the porch. He landed on the stair's dead with his eyes open. Lorenzo looked at him with his gun still in his hands.

"Come one now," yelled Lorenzo as the police sirens got closer.

They ran to the truck and drove off. Kenny saw them pull off and ran out the back door where he found Rock dead. He pulled his body off the porch to the middle of the back yard shaking his head as he ran to the woods. He turned around to see the house collapse to the ground. Kenny pulled his phone out and called Alex.

"Pick up, pick up, pick up," yelled Kenny into the phone.

"Yea, it's not the time Kenny. Sammy's been shot."

"What do you mean shot?" said Kenny. "When?"

"About an hour ago."

"Fuck," Kenny yelled.

"Why are you calling me back to back?"

"They burned the house down and Rock and Steve are dead."

Alex yelled in the phone, "What you mean the house is burnt down and Rock and Steve are dead?"

"They set the house on fire to get us out. Then they shot the house up. I told Rock not to run but he did anyway and got himself killed."

"Kenny, where are you now?" asked Alex.

A few blocks over when they pulled off. I ran in the woods and got out of there before the police came.

"Stay put Kenny. I'm on my way there to get you now." Alex walked back in the room where Sammy was at. Sammy looked at him and said, "what happened now?"

As he sat in the chair getting stitched up, Alex said, "they burnt the house down. Rock and Steve are dead. I'm going to get Kenny now."

Sammy looked at him and said, "Fuck", jumping up and kicking the chair over. "I want her fucking dead now. Alex, anybody who is dealing with her from this point on is an enemy of ours. Alex, pass me the phone before you leave.

"Who are you calling?" said Alex.

"Frankie," he replied, continuing with his call. "Hello Frankie, it's Sammy. We need to talk."

Frankie took a seat by the window and said, "about what?"

"Let's just meet somewhere and talk face to face not over the phone. How about you meet me at the Gold Room tomorrow night around 7:30p.m.?"

"I'll be there," said Frankie.

After hearing those words, Sammy hung up the phone.

SAYNOMORE

Chapter Forty-Six

Elisha looked at the men outside of the bar. It was three of them and two police officers. It was midnight. He looked at Shawn and said, "I'm not going to tell Jamila we ain't go through with it because two officers are standing outside with them."

Shawn said, "Jamila said if you're standing with them you going to die with them. Let's get this over with." Shawn checked his AR-15 and looked at Elisha as he checked his gun. Then he got out of the car and went his way. Elisha watched him as he was waiting for a sign from Shawn. That's when he heard the gunshots. He ran back to the car with Elisha right behind him. Once they were in the car, they were gone like they never were there.

*****

"This is Barbara Smith with Channel 7 Action News. We are here downtown Manhattan on 10th street where two police officers were gunned down last night. It's no secret it's been an ongoing war over the last year, leaving dead bodies behind in a river of blood. To follow, bodies of Mafia families are being found in garbage dumpsters and floating in the Hudson river. The mayor is calling this the worst year in New York City, ever. If you look behind me at the crime scene, you will see broken glass and dried-up blood on the pavement. The effect of this war left two NYC police officers dead outside of this bar downtown Manhattan. Hold on, I have Jessica Roberson coming on."

"Barbara, I'm standing outside of the Pay Your Way strip club in the Bronx, where last night around 10:30, it was shot up and four people were killed and two injured. They said it was four people that came in there. A witness said one was a female. The assailants started shooting up the place leaving four dead. Back to you Barbara."

Sammy was sitting down watching the news cast when Alex walked in the door with Kenny. He looked at him and said, "you told me you killed her. You told me she was dead. Last night I was almost killed. My house is burnt down, and my bar was shot up. Two police officers who worked for me are dead now along with nine of my men."

Kenny looked at Sammy and said, "I saw her body lying on the ground. I shot her myself."

Sammy got up yelling, "So HOW THE FUCK DID I GET SHOT IF SHE WAS DEAD KENNY? HOW THE FUCK MY HOUSE GET BURNT DOWN KENNY?" Sammy took his gun and said, "This is how you kill a muthafucker."

Kenny looked at him as Sammy pointed the gun at his head and pulled the trigger. He shot Kenny until his clip was empty. Then he said, "get his ass out of my site." He sat back down and said, "Alex, call a meeting with all of the families. We need to talk ASAP."

*****

Jamila walked away from the T.V. After seeing the news cast, her phone went off. She saw it was Frankie calling her.

"Hello."

"Jamila you must be doing something right. Sammy just called a meeting with all families tomorrow night at the Gold Room," said Frankie.

"What's the Gold Room, Frankie?" asked Jamila.

"It's a place Jamila where we all meet up at to get clarification on misunderstandings."

"So, I'm guessing this meeting is about me huh?" asked Jamila.

"Nine times out of ten, it is Jamila," said Frankie. "I'm trying to have you pulled in there with us so they can hear your side of the story. So, be expecting a call from me in a little while, ok?"

"I'll be waiting, Frankie."

Jamila hung up the phone and walked away. She went to her window and looked out. She had men walking her yard with dogs and two in the house and warehouse. She had a stress reliever in each hand as she contemplated her next move.

Chapter Forty-Seven

Sammy had two lines of cocaine on his table and a bottle of Brandy half empty. As he sniffed the lines of cocaine, he took shots of Brandy. He had two female strippers in front of him. He watched as they kissed each other and rubbed on each other's bodies. He wasn't in his right state of mind. Everyone who came to talk with him, he kicked out the room. The room had dim lights the color red. One of the girls walked up to him and started to kiss him on the neck. She took the dollar bill he had rolled up and sniffed one line of cocaine he had on the table. She picked up the bottle of Brandy and took a mouth full of it and went to kiss on Sammy. As the liquor was spilling out her mouth and rolling down Sammy's face, she then dropped to her knees and started to unbutton his pants. She pulled his dick out and put it in her mouth Sammy closed his eyes and leaned back. That's when the other girl walked up to him and started kissing on him. He opened his eyes and started sucking on her nipple as his hands were all over her body. He looked down at the girl sucking his dick. He pulled her up. She looked in his eyes then she grabbed his dick with one hand and put it inside of her. She let out a light moan as she was riding him. He picked up his bottle of Brandy and took a big gulp. He saw his gun on the table and told the other girl to sit on the table and opened her legs. She looked at him as he picked up his gun and put the nose of it in her pussy and started to fuck her with it. She was screaming out of pain as he was ramming it in her. He started to think about Jamila and started to fuck her harder and harder with it. She was begging him to stop as blood started to come out of her. He pushed the one girl off his dick then he looked at both of them and yelled, "Get the fuck out now." They grabbed their clothes and ran out the room. He took the bottle and threw it into the wall breaking it. Then he poured more cocaine on the table and dropped his face in it and sniffed as much as he could. Then he fell back in his chair with his eyes closed. He yelled to the top of his lungs as he looked up at the ceiling.

SAYNOMORE

Chapter Forty-Eight

When Frankie called Jamila back, he gave her the address where the meeting was being held and told her that she was only allowed to have three men with her. And when they talked, they were to be outside the door with the rest of the men that will be there. Only the head and number two were allowed in the room. The meeting was at 8pm. And all families agreed to have her there to try and resolve this war with the LaCross and Lenacci families. This was her first-time meeting everyone and she wanted them to see her as a real boss bitch.

She had two guns, a baby 9mm and a .38. Her hair was combed down past her shoulders. She had on a power dress all black that was hugging her body with open toes shoes on all black with red on the bottom. She was wearing a black mink coat with diamond earrings. She looked like a real boss bitch who played no games. Lorenzo, Nick and Shawn were waiting on her outside. When she walked out the door to the Mercedes Benz, Lorenzo opened the back door for her and sat next to her as they drove off.

"Jamila you good?" asked Lorenzo

"Yea, I'm just getting my thoughts together because I know they are going to be looking at me as the bad guy," said Jamila.

"Fuck them then Jamila," said Lorenzo. "Just stay cool and make sure you have your gun cocked and ready. All of you. We can't take no chances with no one."

When they pulled up, Jamila saw Jason and his men walking in along with Sammy, Alex and a few other guys with some people she had never seen before.

That's when she saw Frankie and Marcus' car pull up. Frankie was waiting for her. She got out and walked up to him and gave him a kiss on both cheeks. He shook Lorenzo's hand and said, "Are you ready Jamila?"

"Yea, I am." replied Jamila

"Come on then," said Frankie

When they got to the door Frankie said, "Jamila, listen, don't pull your gun out and no threats in this room. Everyone is on neutral grounds." Frankie opened up the door and all eyes were on Jamila. She didn't pay them no mind. Her and Sammy locked eyes with each other.

"Everyone," Frankie said, "this is Jamila of the LaCross family." He introduced her to everyone and the families before taking his seat. She sat next to him at the table.

Chris Power got up and said, "We are here to come to an understanding, so we can end this war between the Lenacci family and the LaCross family. It's been too much blood spilled and now police officers. It's all over the news."

"So, Sammy, what are your terms to end this war?"

"With her in a box. She killed Tony and Sunnie. I want my blood back," said Sammy as he looked at Jamila.

Chris looked at her and said, "Jamila, do you have anything to say?"

"Fabio been told Tony we will not pay you or anybody else anything. Tony kept pushing up with his threats and he ended up in a pine box behind them. Sunnie was just a victim, I lost a lot of men and you lost a lot of men. You shot at me and I shot back. I'm in Queens. I took over where Fabio left off at. You want to end this war?" Said Jamila as she looked at Sammy with the look of a Black Mamba snake. "If you tell Sammy to stay where he's at and I'll stay where I'm at. Because as you can see, I don't back down. And my bite is just a little bit harder."

Sammy got up and said, "I don't know who the fuck you think you are but I'm Sammy Lenacci." Jamila just looked at him with a smile on her face. "Tony was the Untouchable Boss, so what does that mean Sammy Lenacci?" said Jamila. "History shows us anybody can get killed."

Sammy looked at her and said, "I'll be in a fucking grave before I break bread with that nigga."

"That's going to be the last time you call me a nigga. I respect everyone here. I understand that nobody knows me here and you only hear what the streets are saying, but I want you to hear my voice now. I'm only dealing with the people Fabio's been dealing with. I'm not coming out of Queens on nobody's turf or stepping on anyone's toes. I'm asking for the same respect that's all. Yes, me and the Lenacci family been at war. Sammy you started this war. You burnt down my business and tried to kill me. So, I burnt your house down and shot up your bar. I even tried to make peace with the Lenacci family before."

Chris said, "When? We haven't heard this until now."

Jamila looked at Alex and said, "I kidnapped Alex a few weeks ago and told him I don't want no problems with the Lenacci Family. But I won't back down from them. Then I let him go unharmed and two weeks later, I had an officer named Omar who tried to kill me."

Chris said, "Jamila, each person at this table understands that everyone has taken losses and blood has been spilled on both sides. Sammy this war is over. Whoever strikes first blood again, will have all of us to deal with them."

Sammy said, "Tony helped everyone here at this table and you're going to let this nigga sit here knowing she killed him?"

Jamila went to say something, but Frankie put his hand on her lap to keep her quiet.

Sammy said what he said and got up and left with Alex not saying another word.

Chris looked at Jamila and said, "Welcome to the Seven. We call it the Seven because it's seven families here now. You just completed it. We been trying to get Fabio for years to sit at this table with us, now you took his seat."

Jamila looked around and said, "Thank all of you." Then she got up and kissed Frankie on the cheek and left.

Chris took his seat and watched as Jamila walked out. Then he said, "Frankie, we invited Mrs. LaCross here because you asked us too out of respect for you. But the comment she made about Tony was a little bit out of pocket. Tony was a bit pushy, but they are the reason we all are here today. The main reason we are here today as the Seven."

Frankie fixed his tie and said, "Chris if you don't mind, can I say something?"

"The table is yours Frankie," said Chris.

Everyone looked at Frankie when he got up.

"Tony Lenacci was the Untouchable Don and that reputation got to his head. Jason, I remember he beat your younger brother to death over pennies and to make a point. And Benzino, I remember he sent one of your guys head back to you over a few blocks you had that he wanted. He killed my friend and his wife because they wouldn't pay him nor let him clean his money through their business. The Lenacci family has been pushing their weight around and now we have a female Don who is giving them what they have given us over the years, dead family Members. Tony is dead now, and so is Sunnie. And the way Sammy walked out of here he soon will follow them. Mrs. LaCross just wanted the same respect she gives to us. For us to give back to her. Yes, she's black, but she's been in Fabio's life and nobody knew about her until now."

"Frankie, if I may?" said Jason.

"About two weeks ago I went to see her at her restaurant and from her security and how she carries herself, I'm impressed."

Chris said, "Frankie, her blood is on your hands." Chris walked to Frankie and handed him a knife and a piece of paper with blood and names on it. Frankie took the knife and cut his thumb with it. Then he pressed it on the paper and wrote his name next to it and handed it back to Chris. Everyone got up.

"Does anybody have a problem with this?" said Chris

Nobody said a word.

"Then it's done," said Chris.

And one by one they left.

Frankie shook Chris's hand and said, "Thank you."

Chapter Forty-Nine

"Alex, we need to make a point to all of them about who the fuck we are. Chris is walking in shoes too big for his feet. Sitting at the head of the Seven and Tony's seat. We need to kill them all with one stone. Chris, Frankie, Jason and Benzino, even Paul. And that bitch Jamila. Kill the head and the body will fall."

"And how do you plan on doing this Sammy?" said Alex.

"Calling the Seven at the old train yard and having some friends assist us on it. There's only one way in the yard and there are trains on both sides. So, when they come in car after car, we light their asses up. And that will send a message out to everyone who the fuck the Lenacci family really is. When we get back, get in touch with Roger and have him come see me, the sooner the better."

Sammy pulled his cigar out and lit it. "They will give us the respect our family deserves, or we will fucking take it," said Sammy.

*****

"Shawn, I need you and Elisha to go down to the warehouse and get eleven kilos ready for today. I have someone picking them up. Also get with Lorenzo and see how the rebuilding of Jelani's is coming along," said Jamila.

"Jamila, you know I don't like to leave you alone." Said Shawn.

"I'm good," said Jamila. "I'm not going anywhere today. Later on, tonight I'm going to the warehouse to take care of that little business, but that's it. I have the support of the Seven families now the war is over. We took a lot of losses but as long as we stay strong. the name will live on."

"Just know I'm always here," Shawn said.

"I know already, now go take care of that for me."

Shawn walked out the room and Jamila picked up the phone and called Frankie.

"Hello Jamila," said Frankie

"Hey, I haven't heard from you in a while. I was seeing how you are doing?" said Jamila.

"I'm good, I'm glad this war between you and the Lenacci family is over."

"Me too." I'm just ready to keep all of this behind me now. Hey, I need to see you." said Jamila

"What's up?"

"Is this line safe to talk on, Frankie?" asked Jamila.

"Yea it is," replied Frankie.

"Ok. I'm running low. I need more powder. I only have one more barrel left," said Jamila.

"Jamila let me make a phone call and see if I can set something up with you and Morwell. Now he's big time. So how much do you have to spend?"

"$3.5 million." Said Jamila.

"Ok. I'll see what he will say and if he says yea, he will want to meet you. So, get ready for a trip."

"Ok and thanks Frankie," replied Jamila.

"No problem Jamila. I'll call you back in a little while."

*****

Sammy pulled up at the train yard with Roger. You saw an old broke down warehouse and trains everywhere that have been rundown. They stepped out of the cars and was walking side by side while the car was following behind them as they walked in private.

"So, Sammy, are you saying you want everyone dead?" asked Roger.

"I want everyone fucking dead," replied Sammy. "When their cars pull up, have your guys kill them all. There's only one I want to kill myself."

"And who is that Sammy?" said Roger.

"A nigga named Jamila," said Sammy.

"Sammy, I owe a lot to the Lenacci family and I will never betray the family trust," said Roger.

As they talked and walked over rocks and mud puddles, they entered a warehouse.

"Now let's just say someone gets in here. Sammy I'll have my men in the corner right there. So, you don't have to worry about no one leaving alive."

"So why do you want everyone dead?" said Roger. "If you don't mind me asking."

"Roger, how close were you to Tony?" asked Sammy.

"I loved that man. He was the last Untouchable Don."

"Well, the female Jamila was the one who killed him and the Seven gave her a seat at the table. Now in my eyes all of them are the enemy and they will pay for his death with their lives," said Sammy.

Sammy stopped and looked at Roger in the eyes. Roger said, "How long before this goes down?"

"You have one week to have it set up."

"It will be done." Said Roger.

"Because this just became personal." Roger shook his hand.

SAYNOMORE

Chapter Fifty

Stepping off the plane, Jamila looked around and saw a black G Wagon with tinted windows, her and Frankie got in the truck.

"Jamila, everything is going to be ok," said Frankie.

Frankie saw the look on her face as she looked out the window at all the people walking around barefooted with wrapped clothes on. The dirt roads had big potholes. After twenty-five minutes there wasn't nothing but trees and fields.

Then the truck pulled up to a big white house with over thirty men walking around with masks on so you couldn't see their face. They all had M-16's, AR-15's, Mac-11's and a K9 team car that rode around the grounds. When the car pulled up a man walked up with a stick and a mirror at the end of it. He checked the bottom of the truck to make sure they didn't have any bombs on the bottom. That was the first checkpoint. They had to go through one more before they could pull up to the house.

Jamila got out of the car and saw a Spanish man walking down the stairs with a white suit on. The shirt was open showing his hairy chest off and he had on black shoes with no socks. His hair was slick to the back. He had a smile on his face when he saw Frankie. Once he reached the bottom steps, he gave Frankie a hug and said, "this must be Jamila?"

"Yes, it is. And Jamila this is Oso, Morwell's younger brother," said Frankie.

"Nice to meet you Oso." replied Jamila

"Come, come let's go see my brother," Oso said as he placed his hand on Jamila's lower back. When they reached the back of the house, Morwell was walking around with a female pointing at the workers cutting up the cocaine on tables with no clothes on. He looked at Frankie and waved him and Jamila over. Jamila was looking at everyone and how they were standing. Morwell had video cameras over every table watching everyone work.

"Frankie, it's nice to see you again," said Morwell.

"Morwell likewise and this is Jamila, the one I was telling you about," replied Frankie.

'Yes, Fabio's wife?"

"Yes", said Frankie

Morwell walked over to Jamila and said, "I'm sorry for your loss."

"Thank you Morwell," replied Jamila.

"So, Jamila," said Morwell. "Frankie told me you are picking up where me and Fabio left off at?" Asked Morwell.

"Yes, I would like too," said Jamila.

"Now you know Fabio would pick up a half a ton of cocaine from me every two months. Will you be able to walk in those footsteps?" asked Morwell. "Jamila we are talking $2 million Jamila."

"What will $3.5 million get one every two months?"

Morwell looked at Frankie and said, "she is moving a lot faster than Fabio. Where's he been hiding her at?"

They both started laughing. "Jamila, I will do 1 ton for you if you can honor that deal every two months."

Jamila looked at him in the eyes and said, "I can, and I will." They shook hands.

"So, come Frankie and Jamila. Let's talk about how the money will be sent." Said Morwell.

"No need to have it sent, Mr. Morwell. I handed the money to your brother Oso once we got out the car and had him count it as we talked about business," replied Jamila.

At that time, you saw Oso come walking in and he said, "Jamila it's $3.5 million on the head."

Morwell looked at her and said, "I can see why Fabio and Frankie took a liking to you Jamila." As they walked out the backdoor Morwell said, "Jamila, so this war I heard about again the LaCross and Lenacci family, is it over and will it interrupt business?"

"As of last week, the Seven had a meeting and the war between my family and the Lenacci family is over," said Jamila.

"Are you sure?" asked Morwell.

"Mr. Morwell with the most respect, why do you ask me is it over and about the business, after I told you it was over?" said Jamila.

"Jamila, I understand you were the one who killed Tony. See Tony was a man who honored his word. I have done a lot of business with him over the many years that passed. But this Sammy, I never liked him. He was someone who wanted to be a boss. He thinks with a child's mind and I would never take his word at all," said Morwell

"And why are you telling me this?" asked Jamila

"Because I'm walking out on faith to a new friendship and business agreement. I have people everywhere and Sammy is setting up a meeting to have you and the Seven killed at the old train yard, I was informed."

Jamila looked back at Frankie and then at him and said, "Thank you. So, when will my shipment be in?"

"By the end of this week. I'll have it to you. After this you will pay for it to be dropped off. My job is just to get it across the border. Your job is to get it where it needs to be. Now the insurance is an extra $500,000, but if there are losses, we take it, not you. And your money is safe."

"Then Morwell I'll take the insurance with the deal."

"Frankie, I like her. Not afraid to spend money," said Morwell.

After the business and some small talk, Jamila and Frankie were back in the states.

"So, Frankie, what are we going to do about Sammy?" asked Jamila.

"Don't worry about that, let me take care of that and you just get ready for the meeting. Sammy done crossed the wrong ones."

SAYNOMORE

Chapter Fifty-One

Sammy walked up to his window and smiled looking at the rain fall then he said, "I'm gonna kill all these muthafuckers for trying us," as he smoked his cigar.

"Alex in two days shit goes boom," said Sammy.

Sammy turned around and walked up to Alex and said, "I'll kill Frankie myself because it's because of him she is getting the respect from the other six families and I know it."

Alex got up and said, "if he got to die so be it. I'll have everything ready. Roger has an eight-man team ready to light their asses up as they pull in. Now they're playing with the cards we dealt. After this goes down, we are going to take over more of everyone's turf and build that casino. We good from here on out. I remember Tony used to say when it rains outside, a dog can't smell a wet body in the rain. I'll stand over her body looking in that niggas eyes and pull the trigger and watch as her brains come out the back of her head. Then I'll walk up to Frankie and cut his fucking throat from ear to ear and watch him bleed out. I'll leave both bodies there for the rats to eat on. It's too bad because I used to like Frankie but, sometimes you have to stay in your own lane and know when to cross the street," said Sammy as he blew smoke out his mouth.

*****

Jamila got a phone call from Chris telling her the Seven is having a meeting at the train yard tonight at six. She made her mind up that she was going to take Lorenzo and Shawn with her and one of the new guys Shawn brought to her a few weeks ago, named Badii. He was Muslim but very deadly. He was young with no understanding. But she liked him because he was quiet. Shawn also brought her Muscle and Loyal aka Young Boy. Muscle was smart and knew how to move and Young Boy was wild and always with the bullshit. She looked at her workers chopping up her cocaine. She made the same layout as Morwell had. She had four tables and four females working at each table with nothing on. She had cameras over each table. She also had four bird cages where she kept her kilos once they were bricked up. And one that she counted her money in. She made Elisha and Shawn top dogs over the warehouse. Morwell kept his word and had the shipment dropped off at the waste plant. Shawn walked up to her as she watched everything from the office window in the corner.

"Tonight, I'm going to have you and Badii with me. Lorenzo, make sure everyone has extra clips. We know it's a setup, but we need to be ready," said Jamila.

"Jamila, if you know it's a setup why we are going?"

"Because we are the new family and if we're not there, it will make it look like it was us," said Jamila.

Lorenzo came walking up from behind her. She turned around and looked at him and said, "We're going to take the black Range Rover. Make sure everyone has their vest on we leave in five minutes," Jamila said as she walked away.

*****

It was pouring down rain. Frankie was looking out of the window listening to the raindrops hit the roof of his car. He knew it was going to be a bloodbath tonight. He lit his cigar and blew the smoke out his mouth as the car pulled up to the train yard. You could barely see anything. The sky was pitch black. Frankie saw the old run-down trains on both sides as his car pulled up on the bumpy road. As the car rode over mud puddles, Frankie could see a few cars in front of him and the old broke down train station. They haven't had a meeting there in years. That's when the blue lights from Jamila's Range Rover pulled up behind his car. Before they made it all the way in, all you heard was gunshots. Chris's car was being shot up. He jumped out and his bodyguard was right on the side of him when a bullet hit him in the chest killing him. Chris looked at him as his body was lying in a mud puddle.

The rain was coming down hard. Frankie yelled, "Marcus we have to get out now." That's when you heard a loud explosion it was Denior's car being blown up. Jamila got out of the car and started to shoot up towards the top of the train. Frankie looked back at her, "Come on."

Jamila took off running to Frankie. Lorenzo went to run and got shot down. Badii stopped to help him. He yelled, "Go with her now. Protect Jamila."

"What the fuck, Frankie?" yelled Jamila as she ducked down on the side of the car with Frankie.

"Jamila, look we need to get Chris out of there now," said Frankie.

She looked at Shawn and Badii and said, "you go get him now and meet us inside," as she wiped the rain drops off her face.

"Frankie, me and you need to make it inside now before we get killed out here," said Jamila.

"Come on," said Jamila looking for Lorenzo and saw him lying face down on the ground. "Fuck," said Jamila as she grabbed Frankie's arm and they took off running to the train station as bullets were flying their way.

SAYNOMORE

Chapter Fifty-Two

"Chris come on we need to go now," said Shawn. Badii looked at them and said, "Y'all go ahead. I'll cover you. We all can't run. They will hit one of us."

Shawn looked at him and said, "on my count 1, 2, 3..."

Chris and Shawn took off running. Badii was shooting up on top of the train. He could barely see, because of the rain. Once he saw them run inside, he put his back against the car and put another clip in. That's when he saw a man running on the side of the building. He took off behind him. He saw the man go in the back door. When he looked in the man had a sniper rifle aimed at them. Badii pointed his gun at the man's head and let out two shots dropping his body to the floor.

Shawn pointed his gun at him, Badii yelled, "it's me don't shoot," as he dragged the man's body to them. Jamila looked and said, "it was a fucking trap. This whole fucking meeting. Whose all here?"

Frankie said, "I saw Deniro's car in flames. Chris said, Jason is dead. I saw his body lying face down. And his men, I saw when they got shot up. They ain't have a chance."

"So that just leaves the Gambino family." Said Jamila.

That's when you heard a banging on the door and Lorenzo came through the door. Jamila looked at him and said, "I thought you were dead."

"No," said Lorenzo but we need to get back out there. I saw Polly Gambino. He was shot, and his guys are dead. I couldn't get to him."

Jamila looked at Shawn and said, "you and Badii go get him. Lorenzo go with him because you know where he is."

Marcus was bleeding bad as Frankie was putting pressure on his wound.

"Come on," said Lorenzo as they went out the back door. Look, it's kill or be killed. Ya ready." As they took off out the back door, Lorenzo kneeled down on the ground and said, "we need to get back by Frankie's car. They are on top of the trains, so stay down. Come on."

That's when Badii was shot in the chest and you saw his body fly across the hood of Jason's car.

"We can't stop. Keep moving, said Lorenzo. Jamila looked at Frankie and said, "I have to get out there. They need all the help they can get."

Frankie looked at her and said, "Be safe."

"I will", said Jamila.

Jamila ran out the back door. As soon as she ran out the door she was knocked down from a blow to the back of the head. She dropped her gun. That's when Roger was standing over her with his gun in his hand. She looked up at him and said, "Fuck you."

"No, bitch fuck you," said Roger. This is for Tony. Get up bitch."

Jamila got up and he punched her in the face and slammed her on her back. He picked her up by the throat choking her. That's when Sammy came up and said, "Tonight, you die bitch."

Jamila's legs were kicking as Roger had her in the air still. Sammy took his knife and stabbed her in the stomach. Roger dropped her as Sammy punched her in the face as she held her stomach.

"Sammy let me kill this bitch now." said Roger.

"No, I'll kill her," said Sammy. "Frankie and Chris are inside but they old ass ain't no threat. I shot Marcus so he might be dead. Get your men and get everyone who ain't dead. Tonight, everyone fucking dies. Go make sure everyone else is dead now. We can't let no one leave alive."

Roger took off running. Sammy looked down at Jamila and kicked her in the face making blood come from her mouth as she rolled over in the muddy water.

"Bitch, I told you I was going to kill your monkey ass," said Sammy as he kicked her again in the stomach. Jamila let out a scream.

She looked up and said, "Fuck you, you ain't shit."

He went to kick her again and she grabbed his leg and pulled him down. She got on top of him and punched him in the face. Sammy took his knife and as she was punching him, he stabbed her in the side again. She rolled off of him. He went to stab her again and she kicked at him. He slipped and fell backwards. Jamila went to get up holding her side as she kneeled on one knee. She was out of breath when she saw a brick and picked it up. Sammy was getting up when Jamila smacked him as he was laid on his stomach. She beat him in the head over and over until he wasn't moving at all. She threw the brick to the side and pushed his face down in the water, drowning him as his body went stiff. She got up and fell back down. She picked her gun up out of the water and walked back over to Sammy and put the gun to the back of his head and pulled the trigger two times. She saw the blood coming up from the water. She got up and Roger was standing behind her with his gun pointed at her head. She looked behind him then dropped her gun in the water.

Roger said, "I let you kill him. If he let you kill him, then he was weak and needed to die. But he ain't going to be the only one who dies tonight for Tony," Roger said. Two shots were let off and blood hit the side of the train station. You saw the body hit the ground and the gun dropped in the water. Jamila looked at Badii with the gun in his hand standing behind Roger's dead body.

"Are you okay Jamila?" asked Badii

"Yea, I'm good," said Jamila as she was holding her side. "Where is Lorenzo at?"

"I don't know, I got shot when we first came out here," said Badii. "Come on let's get back inside Jamila."

Badii helped Jamila inside. Once inside, she saw Polly laying on the floor next to Chris. Frankie looked up and said, "Lorenzo, get the truck hurry up," he yelled "We need to get them Medical treatment now."

Jamila laid down on the floor next to Chris. Badii held her hand.

"Where is Sammy at?" said Chris

"Dead. Jamila killed him," said Badii.

That's when Lorenzo pulled the Range Rover up and help them all in the truck.

*****

Two weeks later Jamila was at the waste plant in her office. The gun she used to kill Sammy with, she had it framed and was hanging up on her office wall. Lorenzo and Shawn walked Chris and Frankie into her office. She was sitting behind her desk when they walked in. Jamila went to get up and Chris said, "Please don't get up. This will only take a few minutes Jamila."

"So, tell me what I owe the surprise of this visit?" said Jamila

"Jamila, me and Frankie owe you our lives. It was a bloodbath that night and if Sammy would have had his way, we all would be dead. If it wasn't for you and your family," said Chris.

"The LaCross family stands on loyalty and I knew who was unloyal Chris," said Jamila

"I never trusted Sammy that night, so I never asked how many people we lost that night?" asked Chris.

"From the Deniro family three, the Scott family four and Gambino family two. Sammy's plan was to kill all the heads and he got two," said Frankie.

"So, who's over the Lenacci family now?" asked Jamila

"We don't know yet but, there hasn't been any word from the Lenacci family or Alex," said Chris.

"So why don't we just go to the bar and pull up on them?" said Jamila.

"That's not the way it works, Jamila," stated Chris. "But we are here to give up this," Chris pulled out a locket and cut his thumb on it and put two drops of blood in it. Frankie did the same thing and they slid it to Jamila with a piece of paper that had three names on it.

Jamila looked at it and said, "I don't understand what this is?"

Frankie replied, "Jamila, my name is on it. Chris and Polly's names with all of our blood in that locket. We all owe you a debt for our lives. When you are ready to collect it, whip the name off the list after the debt is paid."

Jamila took the locket and paper and tore it in half and threw the locket in the trash. She then said, "I'm not holding anything over your head. What we did was out of loyalty. There's no doubt or debt that needs to be paid."

Chris looked at her and said, "No matter the day or night when you need me. I will be there."

Frankie said, "Me too."

Jamila nodded her head as she looked at Frankie and Chris as they got up and walked out her office.

SAYNOMORE

Chapter Fifty-Three

"It was quiet out here, very peaceful," said Frankie as he was sipping on his drink. I can't remember the last time I was out here, but the feelings the same as it was yesterday. Music playing, stars out and couples holding hands as they walked the streets. You will never see this in New York City.

"So, I heard that Sammy is dead, and the Lenacci family took a lot of losses over the year and a half."

"Yea, Sammy is dead. Two holes in the back of his head and so is Sunnie and a lot of others from the Lenacci family," said Frankie. "But the LaCross family also took a lot of losses. It was the worst war in Mafia history. The Lenacci family just couldn't do it without Tony, and Sammy led them into a horrible defeat and a lot of deaths. Jamila proved she deserved a seat with the Seven. A black female Don, the first in history who is very respected in NYC who made a name for herself."

"Frankie, I used to sit in that chair right there and watch the news, and every day I saw body counts more people being killed, kidnappings, shoot outs, and police killings. I asked myself if I was a coward to run away and not stand my ground," said Fabio as he turned around and looked at Frankie.

Frankie got up and walked to Fabio and said, "All the brave men are dead, but you still stand." Frankie picked up his coat off the back of the chair and said, "Paris is beautiful Fabio. NYC would have left you in a pine box." As he walked out the door with Marcus, he turned around and said, "She made sure your family name lives on."

*****

"Alex, Tony is dead. Sunnie and Sammy are dead also behind this war and you're still talking about killing Jamila? We lost, accept it. Why risk the rest of our lives? We need to find a way to make peace with the rest of the families before we join the rest of the fallen brothers," said Vinnie.

Alex looked at him and said, "I'm the Don not you. Yet this war is over when I say it over. Does everyone in this fucking room understand that? And Vinnie don't ever fucking question me again or you and Tony will be seeing each other again very soon."

"Do you know what the greatest trick was the devil made people believe?"

"It was to make them think he wasn't real. So, I'll say what I need to say to get us out of this eggshell Sammy put us in. If I know Chris like I think I know him, he's going to come see us with everyone with him. So, we all need to be ready because it can go either way from this point on," Alex said as he walked the floor.

*****

"Lorenzo, how many kilos do we have ready and why is there only three workers at that table? Where is Alexis at?"

"We have thirty-four kilos ready from today and Alexis to my understanding came down with the flu, so Shawn told her not to come in. He ain't want to risk the other workers getting sick."

"Get Shawn and meet me in my office. I want the cameras ran back on that table now. That just don't sound right to me. She was fine yesterday. I want to know who searched them before they left. And I want a count on all the kilos from this week now."

Walking off to her officer Jamila was standing in front of her monitors looking at the video tape from yesterday. When Lorenzo and Shawn walked in, Jamila had her hands behind her back.

"Can you tell me what's wrong with this picture?"

"Do ya see what I see? Alexis is high. Look at how she is moving. Pause the video tape. Look at her right hand."

Jamila played the tape then paused it again. "Look at her. She is walking off from the table and putting my cocaine in her fucking pussy. Shawn since you gave her the day off, you go bring her ass here now. Lorenzo, have Elisha count my shit now." That's when there was a knock at the door.

"Who is it?"

Lorenzo opened the door that's when Badii walked in the door with Oso.

"Oso, I ain't know you were coming. Why ain't you call me?"

"Jamila sometimes it's best not to call and just show up. And you shaved your head."

"Yes, it's a new look."

"How are you doing Lorenzo?"

"I'm good Oso and yourself?"

"I'm fine. Jamila, can we talk in private?"

"Sure, Lorenzo. Take care of what I asked ya to do."

As they walked off Jamila closed the office door.

"Can I get you something to drink? Water, wine or something stronger?"

"Water would be just fine. So, Jamila, I came here because my brother heard what happened with you and Sammy. To be honest, he didn't know if you were going to pull it off. That showed him you are a very smart thinker and he wanted me to ask you would you like to open up the very first casino in New York City. He has a few connects and he wants to partner up with you on this project. And if you say yes, he's agreed to cut the cost by twenty percent."

"And when does this project supposed to take place?"

Within the next few months Jamila.

"And how long do I have to think about this?"

"I need an answer today because after my visit with you, I have to go see someone else."

"Sure, let him know it would be my honor."

"Jamila, I was coming in. I saw your set up. It's very impressive."

Jamila let out a light laugh. "Yes, I got the idea from your brother. Come, let me show you around."

Walking out of her office, she showed him the cages. That's when she saw Shawn come in with Alexis.

"I'm sorry Oso, I have to take care of something." The look on Jamila's face gave Oso a funny feeling.

"Jamila, do you mind if I watch?"

"No, I don't. Alexis sweetheart, how are you feeling?"

A little better now."

Oso watched as Jamila talked while placing her hand on Alexis' lower back.

"Come on beautiful, we have a meeting and I'll let you go home afterwards. Shawn, have everyone meet me in the chemical room for this meeting."

"I want everyone to hear my voice. When I started this family, it was on the foundation of loyalty first, honor and respect. I pay everyone here very well. From the table workers $700 a week. From the door men $1500 a week plus bonuses."

Walking around on the floor looking at everyone Jamila stopped in front of Alexis.

"But see this beautiful child who I welcomed in my family decided to steal from me."

"I'm sorry Jamila I swear," falling to her knees shaking out of control. "Please Jamila Please."

"Now you're sorry Alexis," Jamila said with a low tone in her voice.

"How long have you been stealing from me? Matter of fact, don't worry about it. See Alexis my concern is, who else knew about what you were doing?"

All eyes on Jamila.

"The three girls at the table with you?"

Walking to the door past Shawn, she turned around fast and with the back of the gun in her hand, she smacked him in the face knocking him down.

"You pussy ass mother fucker. You must have forgotten about our talk in the limo. Bitch, you ain't think I wasn't going to review all the video tapes," Jamila pointed the gun at his face yelling at him.

"I watched the video before ya walked in my damn office. Badii, Young Boy, tie this pussy as nigga up."

Young Boy smacked him in the face again, "Fucking scum."

"Alexis, who the fuck else knew you was stealing from me?"

"I'm sorry, please don't kill me Jamila." Alexis cried.

"Who said anything about killing you? I'm not going to kill you. I told you. I'll let you go home. Now go sit at the table over there. Lorenzo, give it to her."

Alexis looked at Lorenzo as he poured an ounce of cocaine on the table in front of her.

"Alexis when you sniff all of that you can go home. I'm only going to be in this room another hour or so. If I was you, I would hurry up. Don't look at me with that sad face. You smiled in my face when you stole my shit. Now I'm smiling as you sniff my shit. Now hurry up."

Oso ain't say a word. He sat back and smoked his cigar as he watched Jamila.

"Shawn, I had a lot of faith in you. But I second guessed myself. I should have killed you back at the farm. But don't worry I'll make sure you have a painful fucking death now."

"Jamila, I ain't do shit," Shawn said, spitting blood out of his mouth.

"What did you say to her at the door? You got it and she nodded her fucking head."

"Alexis hurry the fuck up before you have your ass in this chair. I ain't playing. Ya better pay close attention because I ain't playing with no fucking body in here. Honduras, why are you still sitting down? He stole from me. Everything you need is over there."

Jamila watched the look on everyone's face as Honduras walked over to Shawn.

"You fucked up. You made my Queen mad." Picking the knife up smiling, he looked at Shawn before stabbing the knife in Shawn's hand. Listening to Shawn scream out of pain.

"I want his tongue Honduras."

"No. No Jamila please."

"Young Boy hold his head for Honduras."

Grabbing his head, Honduras jammed the knife in his mouth cutting his tongue out.

"Look at all the blood. Don't worry Shawn it's coming out."

Shawn was kicking and screaming out of pain as blood poured out his mouth. Alexis passed out hearing Shawn scream with her face in a pile of cocaine.

"Now I want three fingers from his right hand."

"Ahhh," was all you heard as he cut his fingers off.

"I don't give a fuck about taking a life. Look at his ass, and I'm still not fucking done with him." Walking over to Alexis pulling her gun out, Alexis looked up at Jamila as the gun entered her mouth. With one tear drop coming from Alexis' eye Jamila pulled the trigger blowing her brains out. Looking at her laying there with her eyes open.

"Eric, that was your table come here."

He walked up to Jamila nervous.

"Listen to me Eric. Next time your table comes up short, you get the punishment as well. Do I make myself clear?"

"Yes."

"Now take this gun, put it to his head and kill him."

Walking up to Shawn, Eric put it to his head and pulled the trigger.

"Meeting over. Lorenzo you make sure this place is cleaned up. Elisha, you and Badii help Young Boy. You are the new door man."

"Oso, are you ready?"

"Yes, I am."

"Good, let me finish showing you around." Jamila looked at everyone. "Listen to me, I don't want to have this talk again. Do I make myself clear?"

"Jamila to win in this game you can't have a heart. If that was me, everyone at that table would have been killed. Because besides Shawn and Alexis, someone else knew what she was doing."

"I understand."

"I like the way you run your business and your set up. You need police friends, judges, and DA's. You have to pay to stay in this game. Everyone pays someone. Never forget that."

"I won't. I'll be in touch."

Jamila watched as Oso got in his limo. As his driver pulled off Jamila said to herself, "I do need cops on my team. I'll have Lorenzo get on that right away."

SAYNOMORE

Chapter Fifty-Four

"It feels like I ain't been in here forever. You can't even tell the place was burned down."

"Lorenzo, how long before Jelani opens back up?"

"It will be open in the next few weeks, Elisha. Keep in mind she has a casino too. She will be running it over the next year."

"So, where she at now?"

"At Sharese Industry's Park. We came here to meet a friend of mine. And speaking of that, here he comes now walking through the door."

"Detective Miller, how have you been?"

Elisha watched as the white male came walking up to them with a smile on his face.

"Lorenzo, I see your father more and more in you."

"I've been good."

"Miller, this is my friend Elisha. Elisha, this is Detective Miller."

"How is it going?" Elisha said as they shook hands.

"So, tell me, what can I do for you Lorenzo?"

"Have a seat Miller."

As he took the seat, he looked at Lorenzo as he was talking.

"Can I smoke in here?"

"Sure, do you need a light?"

"No, I have one."

"Here's the thing Miller, my family needs friends. Ones we can trust. That will gladly take $10,000 a month."

"What type of friends are we talking about Lorenzo?" Miller said as he pulled his cigarette.

"Judges, DA's, officers."

"I have a few friends. Now this payment is to make sure you and your family don't get fucked with. And I will be expecting this payment every month on the 5th. It's going to be $50,000 a month."

"I can do that."

"Good, when I heard there was a black female Don in New York City, I ain't go for it at first but shit, look where I'm sitting now. So where is this Jamila I heard so much about?"

"She is taking care of some other business right now. Here's the first payment: $50,000 all 100's." Miller reached for the envelope as Lorenzo handed it to him. Looking inside making sure everything was there. Miller looked at Lorenzo and said, "I'll be in touch this week sometime."

Putting his cigarette out, Miller got up and walked out.

"Lorenzo, do you trust him?"

"Yea, I do Elisha. He was friends with my family for years. Come on let's get back to the waste plant.

*****

"Jamila you come a long way from the first time we met. Now that you have your own family and this war is over, let me go over the rules with you," said Frankie.

Watching Frankie and listening to his every word, Jamila nodded her head, "I'm listening."

RULE #1, Never get involved with family-on-family beef.

Rule #2 Never set up a meeting for two families if they are at war because you will be the one, they look at thinking you are setting them up.

Rule #3: Never disrespect anyone's turf, set up meetings or move anything without their blessing.

Rule #4: No Rats. We can get our hands on any paperwork.

Rule #5: There will be no disrespect from anybody at the meeting for the Seven at all.

Rule #6: Always put the mafia first.

Rule #7: and this is very important Jamila. Always honor the locket.

Rule #8: Nobody is bigger than the mafia.

"See Jamila, Tony made the way for us, but he forgot about rule #8 and it cost him his life. Not because you killed him. He never wanted bodyguards with him. He had his foot on everyone's neck.

After the first two attempts on his life and they missed both times, he had their family killed mother, father, son, daughter, brother, sister and cousin. That's when he got the name the Untouchable Don. Now you are walking in his footsteps, but you are going to move smarter than him. The Mafia can make you or break you, it's up to you."

"Frankie, I have killed more people in my family, from friends to enemies, over a man I truly loved. There's no turning back for me now. There's too much blood on my hands and I owe you so much. Thank you for walking with me this whole time. It's because of you I made it this far. So, what are we going to do about the Lenacci family?"

"I don't know Jamila. That has not been talked about yet, but they will pay for the blood their family spilled. Their voice ain't as strong as it once was. You know I really wish I could have seen Sammy's face right before you killed him. Nothing would have given me more pleasure. I never liked his ass. But hey, now he's just a dead man with the rest of them who undermined you, Jamila."

"Frankie, Thank you again. But I have to run. I will see you soon."

"You know where to find me Jamila."

"I do."

SAYNOMORE

Chapter Fifty-Five

"Alex someone here to see you."

"Who is it?"

"Chris Teliono."

Alex put his drink down and looked at Vinnie.

"Let him back here," he said as he fixed his tie. Chris walked in the back room at the bar with four of his men.

"Chris, it's good to see you."

"Is it? I thought you wanted me dead like Sammy?"

"No, I was thinking, how can I clean this mess up Sammy left?"

"You mind if I sit Alex?"

"No, please have a seat."

"I'm not going to act like I like you because I don't. So, I'll get to the point. For starters, your family lost their seat at the table. You're not removed from the table but shit your voice don't matter no more. What I want to know is did you know Sammy was setting us up to get killed?"

"I didn't have a clue."

"I find it real fucking hard to believe that his number two ain't no shit."

"So, you come by here to tell me we lost our seat at the table. And to see if I knew anything about what happened that night? Mr. Teliono, I respect the loss of our seat, but you will not come in my place of business and call me a liar."

"I don't give a fuck who you are. Alex. How many owners this bar had in the last year? Don't make the list of the use to be owners. Just know you are on thin ice and it's started to crack already. Now have a nice fucking day."

Chris got up and walked off without saying another word. Alex just looked at him. "I hate that son of a bitch," he said under his breath.

*****

"Chris, Mrs. LaCross is here to see you."

"Let her know I'll be right out."

"Mrs. LaCross, he said he will be right out."

"Ok, Thank you!"

"You're welcome."

Looking around at Chris's house, Jamila couldn't believe how nice it was from the marble floors to the mirror, the paintings on the walls, the double windows. The house was beautiful.

Chris asked Jamila to come over his house no later than 6pm. There was somewhere he wanted to take her too. And to make sure she was dressed up for the event.

It was 7:30 when Jamila and Chris walked into the ballroom. Chris had a personal invitation from the mayor himself. It was a celebration in his honor of his accomplishments.

"Jamila, take my hand, our seats are on the second range." Chris looked at her with a smile on his face walking from table to table taking pictures and shaking hands, as Jamila was talking about the mayor himself as he passed for photographers with the guess.

Jamila just watched from the top of the ornate stairs discreetly eyeballing the mayor. She wore an all-black dress with a slit hemline up her right leg. The dress hugged her body displaying her hourglass figure. Her hair was pulled tightly into an elegant bun with stray curls. In the front she had on a diamond tennis bracelet with a matching necklace on. Black open toes heels completed the outfit.

"Chris, this place is beautiful from the pictures on the wall and all."

"Jamila, those pictures are dated back to the 1900's or earlier. Everyone you see here is rich and powerful. Come on, we have a private booth reserved for us over here."

She was about to take her seat when she noticed a stranger approaching them.

"Hello. How are you doing this evening?"

"Good and yourself?"

"I'm doing good this evening, enjoying the event. Allow me to introduce myself. My name is Justin Love," as he extended his hand out to shake hers.

She took his hand and replied, "Jamila LaCross Nice to meet you."

"Mr. Teliono, how are you doing tonight?"

"I'm doing good Justin."

"So, are you here alone?"

"No, I came here tonight with a few of my colleagues."

Well Mr. Love, you should be getting ready to take your seat. The mayor is about to deliver his speech."

"Yes, I should. Take care Mr. Teliono."

"You too."

"Who was he?"

"An old friend of mine, son. Born rich never got his hands dirty."

"Chris you never told me why you wanted me to come here with you tonight?"

"Jamila, you know the saying: a favor for a favor?"

"Yea, I do," looking at Chris when she said that. "Well, someone is calling in for a favor tonight and you will see him in a few."

"May I have your attention. Mayor Oakland is about to deliver his speech," everyone started clapping.

"As I stand here tonight, I'm looking into the faces of law enforcement officers' men and women. I set my goals a year ago to lower the crime rate, end violence and curb drug trafficking. And you know what, we did it. The judges, DA's and law enforcement officers stayed ten toes down with me and we did it as a team. Not I, but we did it. So, this is not an accomplishment that I achieved, but one that we achieved together as a team. One that we accomplished together as a whole unity of believers. So, I'm asking that everyone here raise your glass and toast to us as a unity of believers who set out for a goal and accomplished it."

Everyone stood up and started clapping. The Mayor walked off stage as he waved goodbye to everyone. "It's been almost a year since the war between you and the Lenacci family been over. Last week Lorenzo paid ya dues to the right people. Now that was smart. Now someone wants to meet you."

"Who wants to meet me?"

"Here he comes now."

Turning around Jamila saw a man walking up to the table with a powerful suit on. Who can tell meant business?

"Chris"

"Jatavious"

"Jatavious, this is Jamila LaCross."

"Jamila, nice to finally meet you. I heard so much about you."

"Nice to meet you as well Mr. Jatavious."

"May I sit?"

"Please do, "Jamila replied

"Last week I received the $50,000 from your friend Lorenzo. Everything you ask for I can do, but I also need a favor."

"And what is that?"

"I have someone standing in my way, who I need to let's just say, get out of the picture. They are costing me a lot of money and that's bad for business. So, I was hoping you can help me with this little problem."

"Where can I find this little problem?"

"You just saw them and heard them."

"And when do you need this done?"

"It's a seventy-two-hour window."

Jatavious gave Jamila a card and the address he would be at. She had until Friday to get it done.

"Once it's done contact me."

"Chris, Jamila ya enjoy the rest of your evening."

"Chris, who is he?"

"That was Jatavious Stone he has a seat in Congress. He's a very powerful man and he always gets what he wants. If you get this done for him, he will back you no matter what."

Jamila looked at the card and placed it in her Louis Vuitton bag.

"Come on Jamila, it's time for us to go."

Chapter Fifty-Six

"Badii, Young Boy what I'm going to ask ya I need done the right way. No slip-ups. And you two are the only ones who know what I'm about to say."

Jamila walked to her bar in her office and got two shot glasses out and placed them on the table in front of Young Boy and Badii. Pouring two shots of Grey Goose in them.

"Tomorrow at 3 p.m. Someone needs to die. They are going to come out the Diamond Pad Hotel. He will have armed men with him. All I need ya to do is hit your mark.

"Who is our mark?" Badii asked.

"Mayor Oakland."

Young Boy shook his head.

"Don't worry I'll be out there with you. Our goal is to stay alive but hit our mark."

"Do you understand me?"

"Lorenzo don't know about this or anybody else. Now listen Young Boy, you are going to come from the right and Badii you are going to come from the left. I'll be inside the hotel just in case someone tries to come in, I got them. M16's and AR-15's is what you will be using. Kill or be killed is the plan tomorrow. I'm trusting both of you. I want your whole body covered. I don't want no skin to be seen at all."

Jamila opened her office door for them to leave. Once they walked out the door, Jamila called Chris and told him it will be done tomorrow before 5 p.m.

*****

"Hey, Tracy. Get the car and bring it around front. I can't be late today. I have a 4:30 appointment with Good Morning New York. Then I have to be at the Town Hall by 6 pm to go over the new system," Mayor Oakland said to his men walking with him.

"Badii, Young Boy, get ready. He's about to walk out now," Jamila said, talking into a mic.

"Shit, pass me my coat, that's my phone. Mayor Oakland. Yes, yes, I'm walking out the hotel doors now on my way to the TV station now. I should be there within twenty minutes. Yes, yes, I'm walking out the doors now Jessica."

"Shots fired, Mayor Oakland down. They are shooting. They are shooting, Tracy. Behind you."

As Tracey turned around, Young Boy shot him, blowing him back with the M16, as John grabbed Mayor Oakland yelling, "Get back inside now!"

As he opened the door, Badii shot John dead in the face. Blood flew all over Mayor Oakland's face before his body hit the ground.

"Police freeze."

Badii took two shots to the back.

"Young Boy, I'm coming, I'm coming."

"Requesting back up we have a 187 in progress on 124th St. in Queens. Mayor Oakland come to the front desk, call 911."

"They just killed my two bodyguards."

Jamila walked up behind Mayor Oakland. The desk clerk screamed when Oakland turned around, "No, No, no wait, wait."

"For what?"

Jamila shot him two times in the face. Blood went everywhere. Running to the door, Jamila saw Badii on the ground. One cop was behind Mayor Oakland's car. From inside the hotel lobby door, Jamila aimed and shot the officer dead in the neck.

Opening the doors, 'Badii, come on. Get up." Jamila grabbed his arm. Young Boy pulled in front with the car. You had a police car pulling up fast.

While Jamila was helping Badii in the car, Young Boy shot the M16 at the police car making it crash into a parked car.

"Come on now, get in, Young Boy," Jamila yelled.

Young Boy was shooting the gun out the window as they drove off.

Chapter Fifty-Seven

It was raining heavily outside as Jatavious sat down to eat. Watching the news, the story was running on Mayor Oakland and how he was murdered in cold blood inside the Diamond Pad Hotel and how two officers and Mayor Oakland's bodyguards were killed. They had no suspects at the time. The story went back four weeks early about the money and 265 kilos that was taken in the raid.

Chris walked in and sat down at the table. Chris was a longtime friend of Jatavious. They both saw things from the same point of view.

"So, what do you think about this?"

Drinking his water Jatavious wiped his mouth.

"It was clean, very bloody. This is going to be a very high-profile case. The FBI will get involved. It will be months before it blows over. Five people were killed, four trained and one very important man. I told you see I will get it done."

"Let her know she's covered and to come see me Thursday morning." Chris got up and walked off.

*****

It was 2pm when Carter walked into the briefing room. You had six FBI agents watching the video tape of the murder of Mayor Oakland. You saw the Mayor walking from the stairs to the front door with his men.

"Stop the tape. Look this female in the black coat and hat. Watch her now. The whole time she never moves until Mayor Oakland comes back inside."

"Keep your eyes on her."

"Agent Moore, play the video outside the hotel. This whole thing was a set up. Shots are fired from the right," pointing at the screen senior director Smith said.

"That's when the first bodyguard went down. Now look to the left. He doesn't even see it coming, the second bodyguard went down. Now here you see Mayor Oakland running back inside.

Agent Moore, play the video of the inside of the hotel now. Here our girl is getting up walking up behind the Mayor raising her weapon as she fires two shots to the Mayor's head. Walks to the door, fires one shot and helps her man who is down. Shoots at the police car coming up to stop them. Now they are gone. Questions?"

"Is there a video of her when she comes into the hotel?"

"Yes, she walks in the back door thirty minutes before it goes boom."

"What about the guys outside?"

"The only time we see them is when the shots were fired."

"What about the car?"

"We found it burned a few miles away."

"What we need to do is find out who she is. If ya need to watch the tape again, go ahead. I have to handle this conference meeting." Senior director Smith said as he walked out the door.

Chapter Fifty-Eight

"Lorenzo, all the repairs are done at Jelani's, right?"
'Yea, you can't even tell the place was burnt down."
"Good, have everything in order. We are opening back up this week."
"Jamila you know a lot of heat is coming down over the murder of Mayor Oakland. Then we just got to move smarter."
"Sometimes you can't say no when someone asks you for a favor."
"We have a support team and a lot of strong ties with the rich and powerful on two levels. Now in this life we need as many people behind us as possible."
"How is Badii doing?"
"He's good. The bullets didn't go through the vest and I've been watching the news. They still don't have any suspects."
"Good, then I have some phone calls I need to make to get some things in line and I'll catch up to you in a little while."
"I'll have Elisha making sure everything is ready with Jelani's and I'll keep you posted."

*****

Jamila walked in the lobby holding a brown briefcase in her hand. She was wearing a pair of brown shoes with some tight dress pants with white stripes going down them and a matching jacket on with a white top. Her hair was pulled up in a ponytail to the back. She was wearing a pair of Louis Vuitton glasses covering her face. There were thirty-six floors in the Moore's Towers. She had an appointment on the 27th floor at 3:35 pm. The towers had a number of businesses in it from daycare centers to WIC offices and even stock offices. The Towers had a beautiful layout. A 27-foot wishing well that had sprinklers spraying water to over 3,000 glass windows she noticed as she was making her way to the elevator where a gentleman held the door for her.
"Thank you."

"You're welcome. So, what floor?"

"The 27th please," replied Jamila.

"No problem."

For three minutes, she stood in silence. Getting off the elevator on the 27th floor, she walked into the waiting room making her way to the front desk.

"Hello, my name is Jamila LaCross. I have a 3:30 appointment with Mr. Jatavious Stone."

"Hold on one second let me confirm. Yes, I see you right here. I'll inform him you are here."

"Thank you."

Before Jamila could sit down, she was called to the back. Once in the back Jatavious was sitting behind a red Oakwood desk. Jatavious was in his late fifties with gray hair and a gray goatee. He had on a blue powder suit. His office was twice the size of the waiting room with glass windows. Jatavious meant business and you could tell by the way he carried himself.

"Jamila, I see you are reading the paper."

"Yes, I have also been watching the news for the last couple of days. It's a shame what happened to the Mayor, isn't it, Mr. Stone?"

"Yes, it is. I see the police don't have no suspects nor witness to the Mayor's murder. Some crimes just go unsolved. Do you think that's going to happen in this case, Jamila?"

"I'm 99% sure it might."

"I guess we will see then. The newspaper said it was a set up very-well planned. What I will say is whoever did it, it was a very clean job. Everything you asked for is done as of yesterday Jamila. You are covered in Queens."

"Thank you."

Jamila went to get up.

"Jamila."

"Yea?"

"Keep a clean face with me."

"Likewise," Jamila said as she walked out the office.

*****

"Alex, this shit keeps getting worse and worse. Mayor Oakland is dead. He was for the Lenacci family. He backed us, now look, he's dead. I'm willing to bet it was that damn Jatavious Stone who had it done."

"Vinnie, relax. We don't know that, and we don't need to jump the gun. It could have been a number of people, but we will make a statement behind this."

"With whom?"

"Chris Teliono will pay for this with his blood."

"And when is this going to happen?"

"When you get it done."

Vinnie walked out of Alex's office. Alex sat on his desk knowing Vinnie was going to make Chris' death very bloody. Picking up the phone he called an old friend of the family. Mr. Washington.

"Hello?"

"Mr. Washington, it's Alex."

"Alex, it's been a long time."

"I know I was hoping to see you sometime today."

"Sure, how about you come to the shop around 2pm?"

"I'll see you then."

SAYNOMORE

Chapter Fifty-Nine

Pulling up to the front gate you had two armed guards. "Roll your window down and tell him Alex Lenacci is here to see Mr. Washington." One of the guards walked to the car.

"Who are you here to see?"

"Mr. Washington. I have Mr. Alex Lenacci here to see him."

Walking off, the guard pulled out a walkie talkie and said something a few seconds later, he smacked the green and white gate and it opened.

As the driver pulled in, you saw cars piled up on top of each other. Backhoes pulling junk cars that's when you saw Kent Washington.

"Kent, it's been a while."

"It has been Alex."

"Come walk with me Alex. What do you see here?"

"Dirt, broken cars, tractors, it's a junkyard."

"It's a junk yard that got more bodies buried in it than a damn graveyard, because people know when you fuck with me you end up dead. Tony, Sunnie and Sammy all let a nigga kill them. You need to move smarter than them. You need to kill her circle, everyone around her. A war ain't lost because you are taking your time to strike. It's lost when you give up. But now you have a bigger problem."

"And what's that?"

"She's protected now."

"I'm not worried about the Seven."

"You should be because Chris introduced her to Jatavious Stone about two weeks ago. He just called me yesterday and told me he has his hand on her shoulders."

"Why would he do that? He doesn't even know her?"

"I said the same thing to myself, but then I started thinking. Alex, watch your step someone dropped a box of nails. What was I saying? Yea, I remember Jatavious lost about $300 million this year because of Mayor Oakland. And they had a heated conversation I was told. Now what's funny to me is that this Jamila comes with

Chris to the Mayor's ball and met Stone. They had a small conversation and within a week the mayor is killed and now she is protected by him. It's not hard to put two and two together on that one. I have someone paying Chris a visit for his hand in all of this. I'm trying to break the Seven up, but Chris will be swimming in the harbor before the week is out. Make sure you just keep your hands clean and stay out of the spotlight. You are the head of a very powerful family now. You still have a lot of people backing you up. I'm one of them. What I need to show you is right this way."

"And what do you have to show me?"

"Someone who had a secret conversation in a parking garage with Mrs. LaCross. One of my guys witnessed the whole thing. He came to me today looking for work, but I don't have any disloyal men around me. And I thought you might want to see his face before I kill him. He's right there."

"Do you see him?"

"The back seat of the car. Alex looked at the crushed-up car."

"You have to be fucking kidding me. My driver?"

"Are you sure?"

Yea, he was shot three times to my understanding. Am I right?"

He was. One to the leg, arm and hand."

"Now, how many people has this Jamila killed?"

"She made it look good to everyone."

Mr. Washington threw his hand up to one of his guys and a big magnet dropped on the hood of the car picking it up.

"No, No Alex. She threatened me and family please."

Alex just looked as the car was dropped in the shredder as he heard the cries of his driver begging for help.

"Come on now Alex. I have to make some calls and you have some business I believe that needs to be taken care of." As Mr. Washington placed his hand on Alex's back as they walked off.

*****

"Hey, you have a light?" Vinnie asked the man outside of Chris's restaurant.

"Yea, I do."

Vinnie looked both ways as the man walked up to him.

"Thanks man. I think I left my light back in my car." As he pulled his lighter out, Vinnie took a butterfly knife and stabbed him in the throat and watched him choke on his own blood holding his body up against the wall until he knew he was dead. Laying his body down, he walked up to the window to see who else was inside the restaurant. That's when Chris and one of his guys came out the back door to Chris' car.

When the door opened, Vinnie shot Chris' man in the head, dropping him.

"Who the fuck are you?"

"For a man who just saw his man get killed and to have a black 9mm to your face, you sure are tough. Let's go back inside Mr. Teliono."

Vinnie pushed him back inside to the kitchen.

"Have a seat Chris."

"I know who you are. Alex sent you."

"It doesn't matter who sent me."

Before he could say another word, Vinnie stabbed him in the neck with a needle making him drowsy. Then Vinnie smacked him in the head with the gun dropping him to the floor. Thirty minutes later, when he opened his eyes, he only had a pair of boxers on and he was tied to his office chair.

I see you are up. So, what business do you have with Jamila LaCross?"

"I don't know what you are talking about."

"So, you want to play this game?" Walking behind him with a pair of bolts cutters in his hand. "Let's play then Chris." He cut his pinky finger off.

"You fucker," Chris screamed out of pain.

"I'll be more than that before this is over. What business do you have with Jamila, Chris?"

With sweat coming down his face Chris yelled, "you think I'm one of them weak links Vinnie?"

"Yea, I know who the fuck you are now."

"I'm glad you know who I am. So, you know who is doing this to you."

"Awww," as Vinnie cut two more fingers off. "You are a fucking dead man you hear me Vinnie." Chris said with sweat and tears coming down his face.

"Not before you Chris." Vinne stated, before jamming a knife in his throat and cutting his throat from ear to ear as blood ran down from everywhere.

It was 3 am when Vinnie left, Chris looked like a carved pumpkin. Vinnie was done with him, taking three pictures of him before leaving.

Chapter Sixty

It was 9am and Frankie was watching the news. The headlines read: Another murder in NYC Mafia Boss Chris Teliono was killed last night at his restaurant with two of his men. Mafia Boss Chris Teliono was beaten badly and tortured from what we were told. He was missing three fingers and his left ear was cut off. The statement we were told was that he lost so much blood there wasn't even half a pint of blood in his system. There was writing on the wall in blood that said, death comes in many different ways. We are trying to get a couple of updates so keep your station tuned in here.

Frankie cut his TV off. Jatavious was smoking his cigar. He had two stress balls in his hand as he watched the news. The look he had on his face was one of death. He was pissed to the max.

"Someone fucked up," he said to himself.

*****

Jatavious was looking at Chris' body lying in the coffin when Frankie walked up.

"Who do you think did it?"

"A dead man Frankie."

I knew Chris for over thirty years. He was a real stand-up man.

"Look around Frankie, you have everyone here. Even Alex to show they support or to hide their hand. Someone is going to pay for his death. I promise you that Frankie."

Everyone turned around when they saw the doors open up. Jamila was walking down the aisle looking like a true boss bitch with Lorenzo right by her side. She walked up to Frankie and gave him a kiss on the left cheek, then she did the same to Jatavious. She put a white rose in Chris' coffin and kissed his forehead.

"It's good to see you again Jamila."

"Likewise, Jatavious."

"How are you holding up Frankie?"

"I'm good."

"Do we have any idea who did it?"

Not yet, but it will come out soon.

"Jatavious you are right," said Jamila.

"Who is that female talking with Frankie and Jatavious?"

"I don't know Walter. She has to be someone just to walk up to both of them with no one stopping her. I want pictures of her and that man she is with."

"Look at her O'Neal. Everyone is walking up to her giving her their respect. She's somebody and I want to know who the fuck she is."

"Jamila you shouldn't have come here. I know you want to show your respects, but you have the FBI taking pictures and I'm sure they have pictures of you right now and Lorenzo."

"Frankie, is it against the law to pay your respect to the passing of a loved one?"

"Right now, Jamila you are just getting into the door and we don't need no investigators on you at all."

"So, are you asking me to leave?"

"For your safety. Yes", Jatavious said.

"Jamila come see me this week at my house."

"I will Frankie. I'll be in touch, Jatavious."

"O'Neal look, they must've told her to leave because they knew we're here. Walter, follow her outside. I want to know what color the car is she's in and the plate number."

Jamila winked her eye at Alex as she walked past him out the church doors back to her car where Badii and Young Boy were waiting for her.

"She even has men waiting for her at her limo. And I'm willing to bet they both are carrying. Walter, make sure you take pictures of them too."

"I'm already on it, O'Neal. I want to know who she is and where she came from."

Chapter Sixty-One

It was 10 am that next morning. You had NYPD, FBI and News teams trying to get comments to find out how the mayor was killed, and the rest of the murders. All news teams were reporting how there was a mafia war and how Mayor Oakland killers were never found.

"Good morning Chief Tadem."

"It's anything but a good morning Detective O'Neal."

"I guess that was the wrong choice of words."

"What can you tell me, Detective?"

"I think we have a female Don running Queens now and she's black."

Chief Tadem stopped and looked at Detective O'Neal.

"I have a fucking Mafia war going on in NYC. Three weeks ago, Mayor Oakland got killed. Four days ago, Chris Teliono got cut up like a fucking pumpkin. And you're going to tell me you think a black female is running Queens? I should drop your ass down to traffic patrol. Get out of my way. I have six different news teams out there. This place is like a fucking circus right now and you bring me this bullshit."

"Chief."

"I'm done talking O'Neal."

"Chief Tadem," Senior Director Smith called.

Director Smith. It's a madhouse out here today."

"Tell me about it Tadem. Come on, I have this press conference and I want you down there with me Tadem."

"Right behind you director."

Walking down to the lobby, Senior Director Smith was ready to make his statement. Different news teams shouted questions in his direction at once.

"Excuse me. Excuse me. I will be taking questions now."

"Senior Director Smith, my question is do you have any suspects in the Mayor's killing?"

"As of right now, no we don't. But we do have a lot of strong leads. Next question."

Over here sir. What can you tell us about Chris Teliono's murder? Is it somehow connected to the mayors?"

"As of right now we have three teams working on the case and we do not know if it is connected at this point in time. Next question. You in front."

"Does the FBI believe this could've been a hit because of the bust four weeks ago?"

"As of right now that is a possibility and yes that has come up. Next question."

"Director Smith, do you believe this could've been an inside job?"

"We don't know at this time, but we are looking into it. Last question."

"What is the law enforcement doing to make our city safe again?"

"We have a plan to take back control of our streets that we are working on right now. That's all the questions I'm taking at this time."

There was flashing from camera's taking pictures of Senior Director Smith and Chief Tadem. As they walked off stage, the expression on his face was a sign of disbelief and stress. It was broadcast all over the news. Headlines read: *Mafia War could have connection to Mayor Oakland's murder.*

*****

Jatavious was in his office still reading the newspaper about Chris Teliono's and Mayor Oakland assassination when Frankie walked in.

"I see you are still reading the newspaper."

Jatavious put the paper down.

"Frankie it's been three weeks since the assassination of Mayor Oakland and four days since Chris been murdered. I want to know who called the hit on Chris, and who took the contract up?"

"You are asking questions that will never be told, not even for you Jatavious."

"They should put a gun to their head if they are going to give up that type of information."

"So, I came to talk with you about this witness I'm hearing about in Mayor Oakland's assassination."

"From what I'm told Frankie, she knows nothing."

"I understand that, but I want her gone."

"She's very protected right now."

"So, are you telling me there's no way to get to her?"

"I'm not saying that Frankie. I'm saying it's going to be hard. Frankie if you are worried about Jamila, don't be. She is covered, I can promise you that. Speaking about her, how is she doing?"

"Good, she just opened back up Jelani's and she's opening up a casino in Queens soon."

"Frankie, a lot of people are going to look at her as a threat. What she is doing hasn't been done before by a female. She has Queens locked down and you don't even know who she is."

"Yea, when I found out she killed Tony two years ago, I knew then she was a problem. But what I can say about her is that she stands on loyalty. I cannot take that away from her."

"I do see loyalty in her Frankie. Come let's go have a drink and get something to eat and talk about this witness and let's see what we can come up with".

SAYNOMORE

Chapter Sixty-Two

"You have a call on line one, Mrs. LaCross."

"Ok, Thank you. Mrs. LaCross speaking."

"Hello Jamila. This is Morwell, how are you?"

"Hello Morwell, I'm doing good. How are you?"

"I'm good. I came to the states to take care of some unfinished business and I have a few hours before I leave. But I'm outside of Jelani's in my limo. I was hoping to see you."

"Sure, I'm coming down right now. I'll see you in a few seconds."

"I'll be in the lobby waiting on you."

"I'm on my way down now."

Reaching the lobby, Jamila saw Morwell in an all-white suit with three of his men.

"Jamila", Morwell said, spreading his arms.

Walking up to Morwell, Jamila embraced his hug.

"It's good to see you."

"Please, follow me upstairs."

"Jamila, this place is beautiful!"

"Thank you."

Walking into her office, Morwell saw her birdcage.

"I see you have a passion for birds."

I do.

Jamila picked up the phone. "Yes. Can I have two bottles of Ace of Spades and five orders of today's special sent to my office now. So Morwell, what business do you have in NYC that Oso couldn't take care of?"

"Sometimes it's best to do things yourself. I have a problem. Have you heard of Kent Washington?"

"I have not."

"Well, he is very bad for business and I have proof. How do you Americans say it? A rat or snitch and we do not need anybody with that reputation being a part of our upcoming project. That will be bad for both of us. Do you understand where I'm going with this?"

"I do. And what's the deadline?"

"There is no deadline. But our project will be in progress in six months. Let him do his part and when he's done with it, so is he."

"I will take care of it."

"That's why I put my trust in you Jamila. So how is business going?"

"Very good."

"I remember when Fabio first got this place and how he was moving. I just knew he would take over New York City. But after the first few years, I saw he was comfortable where he was at. But you, I see you want more, *much more*."

That's when there was a knock at the door.

"Hold on Mr. Morwell." Jamila opened the door and the waiter brought in their food.

"Please, sit everything on the table, and that will be all."

"Can I smoke in here?"

"Yes, you can. I do want more Morwell. I want more than just Queens. I want the whole city."

"And if you put your trust in me, I will help you get it Jamila. You can't have a heart in this life or it will get you killed. And know who your true friends are. Because you only have one. Never forget that."

"And who is this one?"

"Your instincts, always trust them. That's why I made it this far in life," Morwell said as he smoked his cigar.

"So how long will you be up here for?"

"I'm leaving once I'm done talking with you."

"Are you enjoying your meal?"

"Yes, it is delicious Jamila, it's that time. I will be in touch."

Morwell gave Jamila a hug and a kiss on the cheek before she walked him back downstairs to his limo.

Chapter Sixty-Three

Jamila picked up the phone and called Lorenzo.

"Hello."

"Hey, get everyone together. I'm having a meet at Jelani's today at 6 p.m. I want everyone here."

"I'll make sure everyone is there."

"I'll see you when you get here."

Jamila called downstairs to the front desk. "Yes, can someone come up to my office and clean it up. I will need a full course meal up here before 6 p.m."

Yes, Mrs. LaCross I will."

Jamila was looking out her office window when Lorenzo walked in the office. She already had the table set up for everyone. When she turned around, she saw everyone coming in.

"Everyone has a seat. First, let me say thank you to all of you for your loyalty. It's been a very hard two years. We lost a lot of brothers along the way, but still we stand. Queens is our city now. From this point on end we are not going to stop here but before I go into details, I have something to say starting with Lorenzo. Lorenzo is the captain of this family. Badii is the LT of this family and Young boy is the SGT. It's because of them three we are where we are right now. Never questioning me when I ask them to do something and they spilled more blood for this family than anyone. I have a lot of great things planned for our family and tonight this meal is for you and ya loyalty to me. So, enjoy it and let me say this, no one should ever contact me. We have ranks for a reason. Let me make that clear. Do not come to me with no problems. Again, I have a captain all the way down to a Sgt. I'm about to start giving everyone their everyday post where I need them at. I'll open up a nightclub called Rude Boy's, a hotel called Destiny's. We have the waste plant already and Jelani's. I'll get up two houses, one to keep and sell out of and one to hold all the money. Every $100,000 the house makes will be counted before it leaves. Whoever picks it up will write their name in the book and will be dropped off. The receiver will write the name in the book after they count it to make sure all the money is there. The same thing will go with the kilos of cocaine. Make sure your count is good before it leaves because you will be held accountable for it. Do I make myself clear? Also, I have to keep a clean face in the public eye for my image. So, from here on out when talking about me ya address me as Red Invee. And when ya come to this restaurant, you will be dressed up looking like businessmen not thugs. With that being said, I have a gift for all of you here. Lorenzo, go ahead."

"This is from Red Invee's heart to all of you for your loyalty. It's $20,000 in each one of these envelopes."

After Lorenzo passed them out Jamila looked at everyone's face before taking her seat to eat with them. Everyone raised their glasses and said to the LaCross Family.

*****

Samantha walked in the lobby at the towers at 8:45 a.m. that morning. She made it to the elevator and was on her way to the office. When she opened the door, it was strange because Mr. Ross was always there before her. She didn't remember the last time she had to unlock the office doors. She let herself in then turned the alarm system off. Then she went and made herself a cup of coffee. Chrissy had on a black trench coat and a top hat. She had on a pair of black gloves and black sunglasses. She made her way to the 13th floor to the investigation office.

Samantha was sitting behind the desk when Chrissy walked in.

"I'm sorry, we are not open yet. I meant to lock the door behind me."

"I'm sorry," removing her glasses off her face. "I just want to ask you one question and I will be on my way."

"Sure, how can I help you?"

"I'm looking for the witness in the Mayor Oakland murder case."

"I can't give you that type of information and I'm sorry, but you have to go now."

Chrissy pulled a black 9mm with a silencer on it.

"Please, I have children."

"What doesn't kill them will make them stronger. Now again, where can I locate the witness?"

"Hold on, I'm pulling her up right now. She is being held at 110 Miller Street."

"See that wasn't that hard." Chrissy shot her in the chest two times and in the face one time, killing her. She deleted the file off the computer and walked out the office back to the elevator leaving Samantha's body lying in a pool of blood.

*****

She was thinking all she had to do was get the witness Jatavious told her about. Walking down the street Chrissy saw a detective car sitting in the driveway. Walking up to the door Chrissy knocked two times. When the door opened Detective Ross was standing there.

"What can I do for you?"

"Nothing," she responded, shooting him two times in the chest.

"Freeze." Chrissy ran on the other side of the door.

"Ross. Ross."

"He's dead, I just want the witness that's all." Looking in the mirror hanging on the wall Chrissy ran out and jumped in the air shooting him dead in the forehead. His body dropped to the ground. She ran to the room on the first floor and saw Jessica in the corner.

"Rule #1 always keep your mouth closed. You cost three people they live today and now yours."

"I swear I ain't say nothing."

"And I'll make sure you never do."

Jessica watched as fire came from the gun as the bullets hit her in the chest. Chrissy walked up to her and shot her one more time in the head before leaving.

Jatavious got a text. "It's done."

SAYNOMORE

Chapter Sixty-Four

Jatavious walked in his office and saw a man sitting down in a chair in front of his desk.

"You must have some pull to be in here waiting on me. So, let's cut to the chase. How may I help you?"

"It's been a long time Jatavious," as he went to stand up Jatavious looked as he turned around. "Fabio."

"Yea, it's me."

"I thought you were in Paris. Frankie and I pulled a lot of tough strings to get you out of here and to fake your death; wasn't easy. So, my question is why did you come back?"

"Do you mind if I smoke?"

"No go ahead. But back to my question. Why did you come back?"

"To take Queens back over."

"From Jamila, Fabio? I don't see how you are going to do that. Within the last two years she locked down more than 75% of Queens. Compared to what you had she is moving more cocaine throughout the city. She has her own loyal Mafia family. She took down the Lenacci family. She is very respected and if Jamila sees you, you'd better hope she don't put two bullets in your head.

"So, you are taking her side over mine?"

"Fabio, she opened a lot of doors for us. I'm not taking her side. I'm just warning you. The girl you left ain't the same one you knew. Queens is her city now, and everybody underground in our secret world knows it. Fabio your family name lives on because of her. Go back to Paris and leave New York. There is nothing here for you no more.

"I'm not going anywhere, I held Queens down. I built Queens up my team..."

"Fabio, your team is dead. All of them. And Jamila killed Cordial because he was trying to set you up. She sent his head to Sammy. Like I said, Queens is her city now. Start over in Paris. I'll make sure you have everything you need out there as far as work. But other than that Queens should be dead to you."

Fabio walked to the door, "Queens can never be dead to me. I did what Frankie told me to do and now that I'm back you're, going to tell me Queens is dead to me. What do Frankie have to say about this?"

"Fabio don't take it that way. He did what he thought was best for you."

"Have a good day Jatavious," Fabio said as he closed Jatavious door behind him.

Chapter Sixty-Five

"You saw the tape yet, Chief?"

"No, but one of my detectives was filling me in about it."

"She good, really good. You can't see her face, hair or hands at no time," Sergeant Smith said.

"Did you check to see if she was in any other old video tape?"

"We went to check and just our luck, they deleted all old video footage. They do it every four weeks and our fourth week was yesterday. Tadem we can't win for losing," he said shaking his head. "Let's go check on CSI. Hold on Tadem. I got a phone call."

"Hello. You got be fucking kidding me. Ok, ok shit."

"Do I want to hear this?"

"No, you don't. They just found Detective Ross and Moore's body along with Jessica all dead at the safe house."

"Now we know why our mystery girl came here this morning. Fuck Me."

"Tadem same MO, two to the chest and one to the head. All three of them. How far is that from here?"

"Twenty minutes away from here."

When they pulled up, you had three blue and whites out there.

"Director Smith let's go through the back door. This is just a fucking mess."

"You know Tadem, we need to focus on the Mafia right now because these hits are coming from one of these families. And when we find out which one, we find our killer. Come on, I don't want to see no more of this shit. I feel my stomach is about to fucking turn."

*****

"Lorenzo, I have another drop off from Morwell. Is Elisha ready for it?" asked Jamila.

"He should be."

"Mrs. LaCross, before you leave can you sign this paper."

Walking to the front desk at Jelani's, "And what is this?"

"Just the food order dropped off for this week."

"Ok, here you go. I'll be back later today. Have my office cleaned before I return."

"Yes, Mrs. LaCross."

"Hold on."

Lorenzo looked around stopping right outside the front door of the restaurant.

"You feel that?" asked Jamila. "We're winning when all odds are against us."

Fabio was parked across the street in a black Infiniti QX 50 watching Jamila as she stood in front of Jelani's. She was wearing a red skintight dress with 3-inch-high heels on. He was staring at her as her dress was hugging her body. Her hair was laying down on her shoulders and she had a pair of Louis Vuitton sunglasses covering her eyes. He also noticed the two-armed men in suits waiting for her at her limo, and the two that were standing with her and Lorenzo.

"Jatavious was right, this ain't' the woman I left. She was now a boss and she carried herself. You can tell."

"Come on Lorenzo, we need to get to the waste plant. I want a count on everything. Call Elisha and let him know we are coming. I don't have time to spear down there waiting on him. I need to make sure everything is ready for tomorrow when Morwell's people come with my drop.

Chapter Sixty-Six

Fabio heard a knock on the side truck window. When he looked, he saw Frankie standing there.

"How did you find me?"

"When Jatavious told me you were here, I knew this was the only place you would go. Did she see you?"

"No, but I saw her. She had five guards around her. She doesn't even look the same."

"She's not the same Fabio. When you left, she was a girl who knew nothing of this life. Now she became a female Don and took your seat at the Seven, the seat I've been trying to get you to take."

"So, this is why you wanted me to leave?"

"Fabio, you remember laying on a bed bleeding to death, fighting for your life? That's why I wanted you to leave, to save your life. I never knew she would turn out the way she did. She took notes and started a family. Jatavious told me what he told you about going back to Paris. He will make sure you have everything you need out there."

"I don't need his plug. I have my own and my own money."

"So why are you out here?"

"Let's talk at my house."

*****

"Lorenzo, when we were outside of Jelani's, did you see that truck parked across the street?"

"Yea, I did."

"You think it was the Feds?"

"I don't know, but I know we ain't being followed so it might not have been."

"And if it wasn't them, who could it have been?"

"It could have just been someone picking up flowers from the flower shop across the street Jamila."

"Yea, I might just be reading too much into it. You know what, I'm not taking no chances," said Jamila as she tapped on the glass window in the limo.

"Yes, Mrs. LaCross?"

"Take me back to Jelani's right away."

"You do think it was the Feds?"

"Lorenzo, I don't know who it was and I'm just playing it safe right now. When we get back, go across the street and see if that car was parked there, while the owner was just buying flowers. I want to know. It's way too much at risk now."

*****

Walking through the doors, Kent Washington looked at Alex with a smile on his face.

"I see you made a point. It's been all over the news."

"Yea, I saw it, so what's next?"

"Come Mr. Washington, let's go talk in the back room. Kent, what would you like to drink on?"

"Brandy, no ice."

"So, you know Jatavious is looking for the man who killed Chris. And you know what, Kent you still have people on witch hunts and they ain't find one yet."

"You're right. I'm ready to kill Frankie and Jatavious Stone."

"With Jatavious out the way, killing Jamila won't be a problem at all. "

"You know what Alex; I think I might be able to help you out on that one. Let me go see a friend of mine. We might not be able to kill Frankie, but I know we can get Stone. If we play our cards right."

"I'm all in. I'm waiting on you, Mr. Washington. Just know, when I make the call, I want the same layout as our old friend Chris."

"You have my word. Come let me walk you out."

"It's a beautiful day outside, isn't it?"

"The worst things happened on the best day Alex. I will tell you that."

SAYNOMORE

Chapter Sixty-Seven

"Jamila, look right there. Who is that outside talking to Alex?"

"I don't know," Jamila said as the limo rode past his bar, going back to Jelani's.

"What I need to do is get in touch with Jatavious and see if we are under investigation. He knows the right people who will talk to him but won't talk to us. We don't know who got who working for them and we have a lot of secret enemies out here."

"Always keep that in mind."

"I never forgot it."

"You know what it's pointless to go back to Jelani's and call Mr. Stone. Alvie don't go back to Jelani's, take me to the towers."

"Do you need me to go inside with you?"

"No, I'll be fine. Just meet me back at Jelani's." As her limo pulled up, Alvie got out and opened the limo door for Jamila. It was 3:25 when Jamila walked in through the lobby. Jatavious was getting off the elevator when he saw Jamila getting on.

"Look what the wind blew in. Hey Mr. Stone."

"Mrs. LaCross, I didn't know you were coming by."

"Yea, I need to talk to you about something that couldn't wait."

"Come let's go back to my office." Placing his hand on her lower back and walking her on to the elevator.

"So how are you doing today?"

"I'm doing good and yourself Mr. Stone?"

"I'm great Jamila. Come on, this is our floor." As they walked through the waiting room to his office.

"So, tell me Jamila. What was so important that you needed to see me right away?"

Taking a seat in front of his desk. "Here's the thing, about two hours ago I saw a black SUV parked across the street from my restaurant. At first, I thought it was the Feds, but when I realized it wasn't, I was not being followed, I said it couldn't have been them."

Taking his seat behind his desk Jamila looked at him.

"Can you find out if I'm under investigation?"

"I can do that. I will work on that ASAP."

Walking to the window Jamila looked down and saw a limo pulling up and Mr. Washington getting out.

"Jatavious, can you come here for a second? Who is that man that just got out of that limo?"

Looking down with his hand on his chin he said, "that is Mr. Washington. He owns the company on the 20th floor. Why do you ask?"

Right before I came here, I saw him and Alex outside his bar talking. "

"You sure about that?"

"I am."

"If he was outside Alex bar talking to Alex that means Alex has something he wants, or Alex did a favor for him."

"No, I really hope not."

"What are you thinking?"

"I wonder did he have his hands in Chris's murder and if he did then, he got Alex to pull it off for him."

"How come I never heard of him before?" asked Jamila

"Just like you never heard of me too. We met. He is a very powerful man, but he knows his limits and lines to cross."

"So, you think he had Chris killed?"

"If he was with Alex there is no question that he ain't have his hands in his murder."

"So how are you going to find out if he did or not?"

"Jamila sometimes you don't have to find out the truth to an answer. You know you just have to deal with it."

"So, we are aiming at Mr. Washington now?"

"No, we going to aim at both of them, but we going to kill Kent and that's for damn sure."

"Is your car outside waiting for you?"

"No, I got dropped off."

"Don't ever let them drop you off anywhere and I'll have my car take you to Jelani's."

Chapter Sixty-Eight

"Fabio, back in 1989, I was thirty-five years old when I started the Landon family. Everyone was against it, but your father and this one black man named Anthony Cotwell who worked as an accountant for Tony Lenacci. There was this one boss who run the Bronx named Timmy Gunz. Everyone had to pay him. No matter who you were. At the time I was a part of a family called Sennotoes. And I had been for nine years. Simme Sennotoes came up short one time with Timmy Gunz payment. He insured me that they were friends and business was business and he was going to talk to him. He asked Anthony Cotwell to come with him so they can make some kind of business agreement. The story was told that Timmy Gunz wanted to make a point, not to be fucked with. He put Simme Sennotoes on a meat hook and had him just hanging there. As they beat him until he was dead. Then they threw his body in the river. When the police found his body, his hands were cut off. He had missing teeth and his feet was gone. The only way they knew who he was because of a tattoo he had on his neck of a gun with five bullets under it. As for Anthony Cotwell, they asked him to come work for them and he refused. Now mind you, I say they beat him and peeled his skin off the muscle and his muscles off the bone. They recorded all of this. Then they took a gun put it to his head and blew his brains out killing him. They sent the tape to his wife and eleven-year-old daughter. Both of them were my friends who was killed. Everyone told me to stand down. I said fuck them. The only person I wanted dead was Timmy Gunz, so I watched him day and night. I saw when his driver dropped him off at the Moon Light Club downtown Harlem. His driver pulled in an empty parking lot to wait for him as he always does. He always stands outside the car and smoke three to four Marlboros. I walked up to him and asked him how it was going. It was my first time seeing him face to face. That's when I realized he was a young kid.

"He couldn't have been more than twenty-three. But my mind was made up. I shot him one time in the chest killing him. I looked around to see who was watching me. No one heard the gun shot. I popped the trunk and put his body in it. The look on his face when he dropped his smoke was like he was pleading for me to help him. I watched as he died that night. When Timmy Gunz came out of the club, I was his driver. He was too drunk to realize it. I brought him to the docks. When he opened the door, I smacked him in the face with a Billy club. He was out cold. When he woke up, his feet were in a block of concrete and I had two cement blocks tied to his hand on the end of ropes. He looked at me one time and all I did was push him in the water and I laid the young boy down next to the car.

"That was 4:30 in the morning. They didn't find him for six hours and obviously, he was dead. Everyone knew I did it and that's when I got the respect from the Mafia families. As for the Timmy Gunz crew, I had them all killed one by one. It was the worst killing spree in New York City. It was so much blood in the streets the newspaper called it The River of Blood in NYC. Then I started my own family called the Landon Family. Everyone who was a part of the Sennotoes family came with me. I've been wanting my own family and my two friends who supported me were killed and I killed the man who killed them. That's how I got the Bronx under my control and it's been my turf ever since."

"Why did you never tell me this story before Frankie?" asked Fabio.

"It was no point to know. There's a lot about my past you don't know about Fabio. But the main reason I'm telling you this story is because Jamila killed Sammy and Sunnie over you. And I saw with my own two eyes the way she killed Sunnie. No man should've died that way. She been shot over you. She lost her friends over you. She even killed Cordial over you when she found out he was trying to set you up. When you left, she went into warfare. The New York Times called it the bloodiest year New York City has ever seen. Bodies being found in trash, dumpsters, even the Hudson River, cops were killed. Everyone who was a part of your death and your parent's death, she killed them. Everyone down to the fucking Mayor, Fabio. Everyone who was a part of the Lenacci family somehow got killed, she took over Queens and locked it down from drugs to gambling. Her name is well respected. Fabio, do you really think after all she's done that Jatavious, the Scott family, Denior family, the Teliono Family are going to let anything happen to her? She turned down the locket with Chris and my blood in it. Everything she did was over you. No one else.

"Fabio, look at me, I'm asking you as the little boy I look at as my son. Go back to Paris. Leave NYC and start a new life. What more do you want? Your family has the strongest name in NYC right now."

"Frankie you ain't ever told me nothing wrong from the time I was a teenager. Can I at least see her one more time?"

"Fabio let it go. Now come on let me take you to the airport and I will be out there to see you in the upcoming months."

SAYNOMORE

Chapter Sixty-Nine

Jatavious walked in Mr. Washington's office.

"Hello, Mr. Stone."

"Good evening. Is Washington available?"

"Let me find out. Mr. Washington you have Mr. Stone here to see you. Ok, yes Sir. Mr. Washington said come on back."

Walking into the back Jatavious thought back how Chris was killed and the man who had him killed was about to smile in his face.

"Jatavious, now this is a surprise," Kent said as he put his hand out to shake. "Jatavious, so what brings you by?"

"Well, my afternoon is clear, so I wanted to know if you had time to play a game of chess."

"I do. I believe the last time we played I won."

"Come on I already have the board set up for times like this."

"Jatavious white or black?"

"I'll take black. What do you think about all of these murders within the last year Kent?"

"I'm used to it. You know how Mafia wars get and now there is this female named Jamila, who I heard has taken over Queens. It's going to be more body counts in the years to come. But what shocked me was when the Mayor was assassinated. Within seventy hours of his speech two bodyguards and one police officer dead. And one officer who was in ICU for four months. Rook to Bishop Jatavious. Now that shocked me.

"Yea me too. I remember following it on the news for two weeks and no arrest. Queens take Rook, Kent."

"Good move, I ain't see that one coming. But then again sometimes Jatavious you sacrifice your strong piece to get a stronger piece. Knight takes Queen."

"You know Kent, Chris was a real close friend of mine and to know he was killed in such a fucked-up way really cut me deep. But, hey, in this life we live people die all the time. And Kent it's not good to sacrifice your strongest piece all the time because who's going to protect your king. Knight take Bishop. Checkmate Kent. A lot of sacrifices were made these last few years and still more to come. You have a goodnight Kent.

"You too Jatavious. You too."

*****

It was 8:30 p.m. Mr. Washington was in his backyard talking on the phone when Jamila walked up from the side of the house.

"Let me guess, Jatavious sent you?"

Jamila didn't say a word, she just looked at him. He put his hands on his head.

"Hey, let me call you back. I think I just met Jamila." Hanging the phone up, that's when he saw Lorenzo.

"I guess this is my last night on this earth."

Lorenzo had his gun pointed at Kent's head.

"Why did you have Chris killed?"

"The same reason Jatavious had Mayor Oakland killed. Because we had the FBI watching all of us. Now even you Jamila."

"I'm not worried about the FBI Kent."

"Why because you think Jatavious got your back. You are under his protection? Let me tell you, I made him rich. I put him where he is at today and everything you did for him came with a price of blood. Now I'm standing in front of you."

"Your demons come back to haunt you Kent."

"And you don't think those same demons are going to come back after you, Jamila?"

"They might sometime in the future, but tonight they are here for you. You made yourself a loose end."

"Who the fuck you are calling a loose end?"

"You are. That's why we are at this point right now."

"So, you think killing me will end everything?"

"I been watching you for the last few days. I know without you, Alex will be destroyed. You are his helping hand. I don't hide behind my shooters. I let you see who is coming for you and right now. I'm guessing you're wondering why I haven't killed you yet? Because I want to know, why?"

"Why what?"

"Why did you told Alex to kill Chris?"

"You know already."

No, I don't. I know what was heard."

At that time, you saw Badii come out the house with three CD's in his hand. Then he said, "Don't worry Jamila we will know soon enough. I believe the answer is on the CD's."

Kent looked at them and said, "I wonder what the headlines on the newspaper about my death will be? I guess you want me to beg for my life?"

"No, I want you to know how it feels to know you're about to die."

Jamila looked at Lorenzo and nodded her head. Lorenzo pulled the trigger two times hitting Kent in the chest.

"You are having a hard time breathing Kent? Guess what now you know what it feels like to die," Jamila said kneeling down in front of him.

"You trying to say something?"

With blood bubbles coming out of his mouth, his last words were, "Fabio is…" then he closed his eyes.

"Jamila, what was he trying to say?"

"I don't know he said Fabio's name before he died. Come on let's go."

SAYNOMORE

Chapter Seventy

"Who was that on the phone?"

"Vinnie, that was Kent Washington and if I heard him right, he was talking to Jamila."

"About what?"

"We will never know," Alex said as he was sitting at the bar looking at everyone around him.

"You think she killed him?"

"I can tell in his voice he knew he was going to die."

"Fuck", Alex yelled throwing a bottle against the side of the bar wall. "You know what put a bomb on that bitches car and that's how we're going to end her story."

"And when you want it done?"

"Yesterday, the sooner this bitch is dead the better."

"Vinnie got up and walked out of the bar."

*****

"Frankie you have a Mr. Vinnie here to see you."

"Tell him, I'll be right out."

"You can have a seat he will be right out."

"Vinnie Lenacci, I see you are here by yourself so I'm taking it you are not here to kill me?"

"No, I'm here to see if we can help each other, with a small matter."

"I'm listening."

"I know last night Jamila killed Kent Washington. For whatever reason."

Frankie looked in Vinnie's eyes as he talked because he knew nothing about this.

"Alex told me to put a bomb in her car. I'm not trying to put my family back at war. I'm not Sammy or Sunnie nor Alex. We both lost a lot of friends over nothing."

"So why did you come to me with this?" asked Frankie with a puzzled look on his face.

"Because I know you can talk to her."

"And say what to her?"

"For the right price, I'll kill Alex. But I need your help."

"And how do I know this ain't a set up on her behalf?"

"I've been in the Mob, Frankie all my life and I never seen anything like what she did before. She took over Queens in just two and a half years. I want to go home and have a peaceful night's sleep for once."

"I'll take a walk out on the limb and believe you. So how can we do this?"

"Now, that Washington is dead, Alex most likely is not going to leave the bar. When he does, it's going to be to go home. He only takes one road and that's 42nd street. We set up a roadblock and light his ass up there."

Frankie looked at him funny.

"If I wanted to set you up Frankie I would trust me. There's no other way the bar has eight to ten men there and his house has more. This way you will only be dealing with four men, his driver and three guards."

"So, when he's dead you become the head of the family?"

"And you have my word the war will end." Vinnie put his hand out for Frankie to shake it.

When Frankie grabbed his hand he said, "If you fuck me on this, I swear I will make sure you have a bloody fucking death. Do you understand me?"

Very clear.

"So, when is this going to take place?"

"That all depends on how soon you can set things up."

"Thursday."

"What time?"

"Be ready at 5 p.m."

"There's nothing more to say."

Then Frankie walked Vinnie to the door and watched him drive off, before closing the door.

Mob Ties

Chapter Seventy-One

"May I help you?"

"I would like a table for two."

"Would you like the VIP?"

"Sure, I would."

"And will your party be showing up later?"

"No, but can you please inform Jamila LaCross that Jatavious Stone is here, and he would like for her to come eat with him."

When he said that the cashier looked at him and said, "hold on one second please. If you would be so nice to follow this waiter. She will take you to your table."

"Jamila, I have a page to go downstairs. I'll be back in a few."

Stepping off the elevator, Lorenzo looked around at all the guests eating as he made his way to the front desk.

"Jackie, I got your page what is the problem?"

"You see that man over there he said his name is Jatavious Stone and he asked me to inform Jamila that he was here and to come eat with him."

"Ok, I'll take care of this."

"Mr. Stone?"

"Lorenzo, how is it going?"

"Good. Would you like to come upstairs to one of the VIP tables?"

"No, I like it down here. Will Jamila be coming down?"

"Yes, she will be. Did you order already?"

"No, I did not."

"Don't worry about it. I will have the cook make you the special of the day."

"Thank you."

"No problem."

Walking off Lorenzo went back to the front desk. "Call Jamila and tell her to come downstairs and call the cook and tell him to stop whatever he is doing and make two specials of the day for Ms. LaCross. Do that right away and have them bring the food to Mr. Stone's table. This meal is on the house."

"Yes, sir."

Jatavious watched Jamila as she stepped off the elevator walking to the table shaking hands with the guest. Even taking a picture with one of them.

"Jamila how are you doing?"

"I'm fine Jatavious and how are you this evening?" she said, giving Jatavious a hug and a kiss on the cheek.

"I'm glad you were able to come down and eat with me. You know I have never been in here before. This is my first time. Even when Fabio owned it. Jamila, Fabio was very business-minded but he didn't make it to the level you are on."

"Speaking of Fabio, his name was the last name that came out of Washington's mouth."

"Why is that you think?"

"Your guess is as good as mine."

"And look here comes our trays."

"Where did Lorenzo go?"

"Everyone is at the post while I'm on the floor."

Looking around Jatavious saw every door covered with two men.

"I see you are well protected."

"I am. My men love me."

"I can tell why you are very honest and loyal to them."

"That's how my father raised me to be."

"I checked out what you asked me to and you are not under investigation. No one is, but you should still walk on eggshells."

"I wanted to tell you my guys call me Red Invee. I ain't want Jamila to look bad in the public eye. That I'm a businesswoman. So, I'm keeping two different identities. Jamila is the business world and Red Invee is the Underground world."

"Now that is very smart of you Jamila. And that is why you are going to go a very long way in this business."

"Shall we eat?"

"Yes."

SAYNOMORE

Chapter Seventy-Two

"Vinnie, close up the place. And how is that other project coming along?"

"It should be done this week."

"Good, I had about enough of that bitch."

"Getting in the car, Alex closed his eyes and leaned his head back against the headrest. Ah, boss, are we going to pay our respect to Mr. Washington?"

"No, his murder been all over the news. That's all we need is the FBI taking pictures of us there. As soon as Jamila is dead, the better it will be." Alex said, rolling down his window.

"Heads up. We got a road block this time of day?"

"Wait, wait, it's a set up." Bullets went flying through the car windows as Alex went to get out, he got shot in the leg, falling to the ground. Shells dropping was all you heard. Alex jumped up and Vinnie was right there with a shotgun in his hand pointed dead at Alex.

"You got to be fucking kidding me. They sent you?"

"No, I sent them, and they agreed if I killed you the war is over. Night night, Alex."

With one pull of the trigger, Alex's face was gone and his body was laid out in blood next to his car. Vinnie looked at the three men in the car laying there dead. And then he looked at Frankie's men and nodded his head as he walked back to his car. The plan went just fine. He knew that at point blank range, three M16's would do the job. They ain't have a chance.

*****

The next day, Frankie walked up to Vinnie in the park next to the lake.

"So, what now Vinnie?"

"I get to rest Frankie."

"It's over with. I talked with Jamila and she will honor her word for peace."

"So, what about you Frankie now? What are you about to do?"

"For the first time in three years, I don't know. I might do something I ain't do in a very long time."

"And what's that? Go feed the ducks?"

"Take care Vinnie."

"You to Frankie," he said as he walked off back to his car.

*****

Chief Tadem walked in the briefing room where you had Senior Director Smith and thirteen more officers.

"Listen up. This is what we got. Seven Mafia families in Brooklyn. We have the Scott Family in the Bronx. We have the Landon family in Manhattan. We have the Lenacci family in Yonkers. We have the Deniro family along with the Teliono family. I don't know how true this is but there's a new family that took over Queens and they are called the LaCross family."

"Who is the head of this family?"

"Rumor has it a female."

"And what's her name?"

"Red Invee. They say she is moving more weight in Queens than any other family has ever done."

"Sir, do we have a picture of her?"

"No, we don't."

"Is she black, white, what is her race?"

"From what I'm told she is black."

"Right now, from this point on I want two teams on each of these families. Pictures, videos, recording."

"If you can get a guy on the inside, that's good, really good. Chief Tadem and I will approve whatever you need to help this ongoing investigation."

Chapter Seventy-Three

Jamila walked up to Frankie and Marcus in the park.

"You know what, Frankie? The last time I was here me and Fabio fed the ducks together. That was four years ago. So, what did Vinnie have to say?"

"He's going home to rest now. And I think you should do the same."

"I can't sleep. Every time I close my eyes, I see the faces of everyone I killed. And it's been like that from the very first man."

"It will go away in time Jamila. You won, everyone is dead. Tony, Sunnie, Sammy and Alex and you are still here."

"It's over now Frankie?"

"It's over now Jamila."

Jamila gave Frankie a hug and a kiss on the cheek. She did the same with Marcus before walking away.

SAYNOMORE

Chapter Seventy-Four

"Who you think she is?"

"I don't know Miller. Did you take pictures of her with Frankie Landon?"

"Yea and the other guy who was waiting on her over there."

"You think she can be a part of the mob?"

"Boatman, two things I ain't never seen before a ghost and a black female in the Mafia. Let's go. We've done all we can do here. We got the pictures of Vinnie talking with Frankie. And Frankie talking with whoever that female was. Now let's find out who she is."

To Be Continued...

Mob Ties 2
Coming Soon

Submission Guideline

Submit the first three chapters of your completed manuscript to ldpsubmissions@gmail.com, subject line: Your book's title. The manuscript must be in a .doc file and sent as an attachment. Document should be in Times New Roman, double spaced and in size 12 font. Also, provide your synopsis and full contact information. If sending multiple submissions, they must each be in a separate email.

Have a story but no way to send it electronically? You can still submit to LDP/Ca$h Presents. Send in the first three chapters, written or typed, of your completed manuscript to:

LDP: Submissions Dept
Po Box 944
Stockbridge, Ga 30281

DO NOT send original manuscript. Must be a duplicate.

Provide your synopsis and a cover letter containing your full contact information.

Thanks for considering LDP and Ca$h Presents.

BOW DOWN TO MY GANGSTA
By **Ca$h**
TORN BETWEEN TWO
By **Coffee**
THE STREETS STAINED MY SOUL **II**
By **Marcellus Allen**
BLOOD OF A BOSS **VI**
SHADOWS OF THE GAME II
By **Askari**
LOYAL TO THE GAME **IV**
By **T.J. & Jelissa**
IF LOVING YOU IS WRONG… **III**
By **Jelissa**
TRUE SAVAGE **VIII**
MIDNIGHT CARTEL III
DOPE BOY MAGIC IV
CITY OF KINGZ II
By **Chris Green**
BLAST FOR ME **III**
A SAVAGE DOPEBOY III
CUTTHROAT MAFIA III
DUFFLE BAG CARTEL VI
HEARTLESS GOON VI
By **Ghost**
A HUSTLER'S DECEIT III
KILL ZONE **II**
BAE BELONGS TO ME III
A DOPE BOY'S QUEEN III

SAYNOMORE

By **Aryanna**
COKE KINGS V
KING OF THE TRAP II
By **T.J. Edwards**
GORILLAZ IN THE BAY V
3X KRAZY III
De'Kari
THE STREETS ARE CALLING II
Duquie Wilson
KINGPIN KILLAZ IV
STREET KINGS III
PAID IN BLOOD III
CARTEL KILLAZ IV
DOPE GODS III
Hood Rich
SINS OF A HUSTLA II
ASAD
KINGZ OF THE GAME VI
Playa Ray
SLAUGHTER GANG IV
RUTHLESS HEART IV
By **Willie Slaughter**
THE HEART OF A SAVAGE III
By **Jibril Williams**
FUK SHYT II
By **Blakk Diamond**
TRAP QUEEN
By **Troublesome**
YAYO V
GHOST MOB II

Mob Ties

Stilloan Robinson
KINGPIN DREAMS III
By Paper Boi Rari
CREAM II
By Yolanda Moore
SON OF A DOPE FIEND III
By Renta
FOREVER GANGSTA II
GLOCKS ON SATIN SHEETS III
By Adrian Dulan
LOYALTY AIN'T PROMISED III
By Keith Williams
THE PRICE YOU PAY FOR LOVE II
By Destiny Skai
I'M NOTHING WITHOUT HIS LOVE II
SINS OF A THUG II
By Monet Dragun
LIFE OF A SAVAGE IV
MURDA SEASON IV
GANGLAND CARTEL III
CHI'RAQ GANGSTAS III
By **Romell Tukes**
QUIET MONEY IV
EXTENDED CLIP II
By **Trai'Quan**
THE STREETS MADE ME III
By **Larry D. Wright**
IF YOU CROSS ME ONCE II
ANGEL III

SAYNOMORE

By **Anthony Fields**
FRIEND OR FOE III

By **Mimi**
SAVAGE STORMS III

By **Meesha**
BLOOD ON THE MONEY III

By J-Blunt
THE STREETS WILL NEVER CLOSE II

By K'ajji
NIGHTMARES OF A HUSTLA III

By King Dream
THE WIFEY I USED TO BE II

By Nicole Goosby
IN THE ARM OF HIS BOSS

By Jamila
MONEY, MURDER & MEMORIES II

Malik D. Rice
CONCRETE KILLAZ II

By Kingpen
HARD AND RUTHLESS II

By Von Wiley Hall
LEVELS TO THIS SHYT II

By Ah'Million
MOB TIES II

By SayNoMore

<u>Available Now</u>

RESTRAINING ORDER **I & II**

Mob Ties

By **CA$H & Coffee**
LOVE KNOWS NO BOUNDARIES **I II & III**
By **Coffee**
RAISED AS A GOON I, II, III & IV
BRED BY THE SLUMS I, II, III
BLAST FOR ME I & II
ROTTEN TO THE CORE I II III
A BRONX TALE I, II, III
DUFFLE BAG CARTEL I II III IV V
HEARTLESS GOON I II III IV V
A SAVAGE DOPEBOY I II
DRUG LORDS I II III
CUTTHROAT MAFIA I II
By **Ghost**
LAY IT DOWN **I & II**
LAST OF A DYING BREED I II
BLOOD STAINS OF A SHOTTA I & II III
By **Jamaica**
LOYAL TO THE GAME I II III
LIFE OF SIN I, II III
By **TJ & Jelissa**
BLOODY COMMAS I & II
SKI MASK CARTEL I II & III
KING OF NEW YORK I II,III IV V
RISE TO POWER I II III
COKE KINGS I II III IV
BORN HEARTLESS I II III IV
KING OF THE TRAP
By **T.J. Edwards**
IF LOVING HIM IS WRONG…I & II

SAYNOMORE

LOVE ME EVEN WHEN IT HURTS I II III
By **Jelissa**
WHEN THE STREETS CLAP BACK I & II III
THE HEART OF A SAVAGE I II
By **Jibril Williams**
A DISTINGUISHED THUG STOLE MY HEART I II & III
LOVE SHOULDN'T HURT I II III IV
RENEGADE BOYS I II III IV
PAID IN KARMA I II III
SAVAGE STORMS I II
By **Meesha**
A GANGSTER'S CODE I &, II III
A GANGSTER'S SYN I II III
THE SAVAGE LIFE I II III
CHAINED TO THE STREETS I II III
BLOOD ON THE MONEY I II
By J-Blunt
PUSH IT TO THE LIMIT
By **Bre' Hayes**
BLOOD OF A BOSS **I, II, III, IV, V**
SHADOWS OF THE GAME
By **Askari**
THE STREETS BLEED MURDER **I, II & III**
THE HEART OF A GANGSTA I II& III
By **Jerry Jackson**
CUM FOR ME I II III IV V VI
An **LDP Erotica Collaboration**
BRIDE OF A HUSTLA **I II & II**
THE FETTI GIRLS **I, II& III**
CORRUPTED BY A GANGSTA I, II III, IV

Mob Ties

BLINDED BY HIS LOVE

THE PRICE YOU PAY FOR LOVE

DOPE GIRL MAGIC I II III

By **Destiny Skai**

WHEN A GOOD GIRL GOES BAD

By **Adrienne**

THE COST OF LOYALTY I II III

By Kweli

A GANGSTER'S REVENGE **I II III & IV**

THE BOSS MAN'S DAUGHTERS I II III IV V

A SAVAGE LOVE **I & II**

BAE BELONGS TO ME I II

A HUSTLER'S DECEIT I, II, III

WHAT BAD BITCHES DO I, II, III

SOUL OF A MONSTER I II III

KILL ZONE

A DOPE BOY'S QUEEN I II

By **Aryanna**

A KINGPIN'S AMBITON

A KINGPIN'S AMBITION **II**

I MURDER FOR THE DOUGH

By **Ambitious**

TRUE SAVAGE I II III IV V VI VII

DOPE BOY MAGIC I, II, III

MIDNIGHT CARTEL I II

CITY OF KINGZ

By **Chris Green**

A DOPEBOY'S PRAYER

By **Eddie "Wolf" Lee**

THE KING CARTEL **I, II & III**

SAYNOMORE

By **Frank Gresham**
THESE NIGGAS AIN'T LOYAL **I, II & III**
By **Nikki Tee**
GANGSTA SHYT **I II &III**
By **CATO**
THE ULTIMATE BETRAYAL
By **Phoenix**
BOSS'N UP **I , II & III**
By **Royal Nicole**
I LOVE YOU TO DEATH
By Destiny J
I RIDE FOR MY HITTA
I STILL RIDE FOR MY HITTA
By **Misty Holt**
LOVE & CHASIN' PAPER
By **Qay Crockett**
TO DIE IN VAIN
SINS OF A HUSTLA
By **ASAD**
BROOKLYN HUSTLAZ
By **Boogsy Morina**
BROOKLYN ON LOCK I & II
By **Sonovia**
GANGSTA CITY
By **Teddy Duke**
A DRUG KING AND HIS DIAMOND I & II III
A DOPEMAN'S RICHES
HER MAN, MINE'S TOO I, II
CASH MONEY HO'S
THE WIFEY I USED TO BE

Mob Ties

By Nicole Goosby

TRAPHOUSE KING **I II & III**

KINGPIN KILLAZ I II III

STREET KINGS I II

PAID IN BLOOD **I II**

CARTEL KILLAZ I II III

DOPE GODS I II

By Hood Rich

LIPSTICK KILLAH **I, II, III**

CRIME OF PASSION I II & III

FRIEND OR FOE I II

By Mimi

STEADY MOBBN' **I, II, III**

THE STREETS STAINED MY SOUL

By Marcellus Allen

WHO SHOT YA **I, II, III**

SON OF A DOPE FIEND I II

Renta

GORILLAZ IN THE BAY **I II III IV**

TEARS OF A GANGSTA I II

3X KRAZY I II

DE'KARI

TRIGGADALE I II III

Elijah R. Freeman

GOD BLESS THE TRAPPERS I, II, III

THESE SCANDALOUS STREETS I, II, III

FEAR MY GANGSTA I, II, III IV, V

THESE STREETS DON'T LOVE NOBODY I, II

BURY ME A G I, II, III, IV, V

A GANGSTA'S EMPIRE I, II, III, IV

SAYNOMORE

THE DOPEMAN'S BODYGAURD I II

THE REALEST KILLAZ I II III

Tranay Adams

THE STREETS ARE CALLING

Duquie Wilson

MARRIED TO A BOSS... I II III

By Destiny Skai & Chris Green

KINGZ OF THE GAME I II III IV V

Playa Ray

SLAUGHTER GANG I II III

RUTHLESS HEART I II III

By Willie Slaughter

FUK SHYT

By Blakk Diamond

DON'T F#CK WITH MY HEART I II

By Linnea

ADDICTED TO THE DRAMA I II III

IN THE ARM OF HIS BOSS II

By Jamila

YAYO I II III IV

A SHOOTER'S AMBITION I II

By S. Allen

TRAP GOD I II III

By Troublesome

FOREVER GANGSTA

GLOCKS ON SATIN SHEETS I II

By Adrian Dulan

TOE TAGZ I II III

LEVELS TO THIS SHYT

By Ah'Million

Mob Ties

KINGPIN DREAMS I II

By Paper Boi Rari

CONFESSIONS OF A GANGSTA I II III

By Nicholas Lock

I'M NOTHING WITHOUT HIS LOVE

SINS OF A THUG

By Monet Dragun

CAUGHT UP IN THE LIFE I II III

By Robert Baptiste

NEW TO MONEY, MURDER & MEMORIES

THE GAME I II III

By **Malik D. Rice**

LIFE OF A SAVAGE I II III

A GANGSTA'S QUR'AN I II III

MURDA SEASON I II III

GANGLAND CARTEL I II

CHI'RAQ GANGSTAS I II

By **Romell Tukes**

LOYALTY AIN'T PROMISED I II

By Keith Williams

QUIET MONEY I II III

THUG LIFE I II

EXTENDED CLIP

By **Trai'Quan**

THE STREETS MADE ME I II

By **Larry D. Wright**

THE ULTIMATE SACRIFICE I, II, III, IV, V, VI

KHADIFI

IF YOU CROSS ME ONCE

ANGEL I II

By **Anthony Fields**

THE LIFE OF A HOOD STAR

By Ca$h & Rashia Wilson

THE STREETS WILL NEVER CLOSE

By K'ajji

CREAM

By Yolanda Moore

NIGHTMARES OF A HUSTLA I II

By King Dream

CONCRETE KILLAZ

By Kingpen

HARD AND RUTHLESS

By Von Wiley Hall

GHOST MOB II

Stilloan Robinson

MOB TIES

By SayNoMore

BOOKS BY LDP'S CEO, CA$H

TRUST IN NO MAN

TRUST IN NO MAN 2

TRUST IN NO MAN 3

BONDED BY BLOOD

SHORTY GOT A THUG

THUGS CRY

THUGS CRY 2

THUGS CRY 3

TRUST NO BITCH

TRUST NO BITCH 2

TRUST NO BITCH 3

TIL MY CASKET DROPS

RESTRAINING ORDER

RESTRAINING ORDER 2

IN LOVE WITH A CONVICT

LIFE OF A HOOD STAR

SAYNOMORE

CPSIA information can be obtained
at www.ICGtesting.com
Printed in the USA
LVHW051304140321
681503LV00006B/137